The Christmas Ledger

Sarah Phillips

Published by Sarah Phillips, 2025.

THE CHRISTMAS LEDGER

First edition. October 27, 2025.

Copyright © 2025 Sarah Phillips.

ISBN: 979-8991996839

Written by Sarah Phillips.

Table of Contents

He's Making a List...

"NO! I DISAGREE!" Cavan slammed his hand on the oak table, sending hot cocoa sloshing from his mug. The dark liquid spread like ink over the grain. Nicholas looked down at the puddle, his eyebrows lifting over the rim of his glasses.

Oh, they're at it again, Martha fretted from the next room. She had stood beside Nicholas through centuries of lists and quarrels — she knew this one was going to be bad.

It had all started pleasantly enough. But it didn't take long—just a few pages into the Naughty and Nice List—before Cavan was raising his voice.

He and Nicholas sat opposite each other at the enormous oak table in the North Pole's great dining room, the thick books of names spread out before them. It had taken four elves to carry in the heavy volumes and gently place them on the table.

"Will that be everything, Father Christmas?" asked one of the elves, slightly out of breath.

"Yes, thank you," Nicholas replied with a warm smile to his loyal helpers.

"Father Christmas?" Cavan repeated, raising a skeptical eyebrow. "Is that what they're calling you these days? Whatever happened to St. Nicholas—or Kris Kringle?"

Nicholas shrugged. "I don't know. But I like the new name. It sounds warm... personal."

"If it's all the same to you, I'll keep calling you Nick," Cavan muttered. "Calling you St. Nicholas"—he emphasized the word *saint*— "or Father Christmas," his voice mocked, "just makes you big-headed."

Nicholas chuckled. "You don't hold back, do you? It doesn't matter to me." He opened a book and smiled faintly. "Suit yourself. Come on, let's get to work."

The firelight flickered across the pages. This particular meeting had taken place decades ago—though neither of them could recall the exact year. Time was a trivial concept to beings as eternal as they were. Humans measured their fleeting existence in years, but for St. Nicholas and Cavan, the passing of a decade was no more than the turning of a page.

They had sorted their way to the D's without a single disagreement. But lately, arguments came more often—and louder.

"Albert Davidson—definitely the Naughty List," Nicholas declared, his finger gliding to the next name.

That was the name that started it.

"Wait, wait, not so fast," said Cavan holding up a hand.

"There's ample evidence against him," Nicholas said, his finger still hovering over the next name on the list.

"Yes, but his sister is the real troublemaker. She's always egging him on, getting him into trouble," replied Cavan as he sat back in his chair and folded his arms.

Nicholas sighed. "Perhaps, but Albert has pulled her hair over a hundred times this year. One hundred. That's not exactly excusable behavior. It's the naughty list for Albert."

Cavan slammed the table. **"No! I disagree!"**

Now, with cocoa creeping into the wood grain, Nicholas rubbed his temples. "Your heart has always been soft, my friend — and I admire that. But justice and fairness must guide us. We've discussed this again and again. Actions have consequences. If children don't learn that now, how will they understand it as adults?"

Cavan exhaled slowly. "That's easy for you to say. You're always talking about joy and hope. I deliver a lump of coal — not much joy in that."

Nicholas met the eyes of his oldest and dearest friend. "But change, the chance to do better — that's hope too. And I don't do this only to hand out gifts. I do it so the world remembers the first Christmas. Hope and joy matter, yes... but so does justice. Together, they show what Christmas really means."

Cavan grumbled, "Still... you bring the joy. I bring the disappointment. You're always hailed as the hero."

"Once again, I must disagree, my old friend. Think of the lives changed because of your work. You've shown countless children that actions matter. You're the true hero, Cavan. Don't forget it. We're two sides of a perfectly balanced scale: reward and justice."

Martha's voice called from the next room, "Perhaps, we should start a new book called, '*Stubborn,*' and put both of your names in it."

Nicholas chuckled and Cavan rolled his eyes.

"While we're on the subject... why does it have to be coal? It's messy. You know I can't bear a mess," Cavan continued.

Nicholas stood and tossed another log onto the fire. "It's not about what's best for us," he said. "It's about what they need. Now, let's move on to the next name before we're stuck here for a century."

The fire roared back to life, sending a wave of heat through the room. Cavan groaned and loosened the collar of his shirt. "Really? Was that necessary?" he mumbled. "It's already hotter in here than the Bahamas in midsummer. You're suffocating me! For someone your size, you're surprisingly cold all the time."

Cavan crossed the room and opened a window, inhaling the crisp air. Tall, lean, broad-shouldered—Cavan's name, meaning 'handsome,' suited him perfectly. He paused at the gold-framed mirror, smoothing a strand of dark hair that had slipped out of place.

Nicholas chuckled. "Every time you pass a mirror, you stop. You just can't help yourself."

"Some of us take pride in our appearance. You might try trimming that scraggly beard of yours once in a while," Cavan said with a smirk.

Nicholas's laughter filled the room. It had always been that way — laughter and teasing. But their bond ran deeper than banter. Cavan had been with Nicholas and Martha from the very beginning, when Nicholas was still just a man who began the gift-giving.

Towards the end of his mortal life, Nicholas petitioned to remain on earth with Cavan and Martha and continue their work of bringing joy and hope to the world. He wanted mankind never to forget the light born on that night in Bethlehem. His plea was granted, and from that moment on Nicholas became something more — Kris Kringle, Father Christmas, Santa Claus. Different names, one calling. And Martha shared in that calling, steady and faithful at his side, while Cavan carried the heavy weight of justice.

Nicholas, Martha, and Cavan — more than partners, family. Their work so in tune they could often predict one another's next move, even their next words. Nicholas brought joy and gifts to those who earned a place on the Nice List; Cavan left lumps of coal as a stern reminder to those who did not.

But lately something had begun to shift in Cavan. It started quietly—an ache in his heart. Then came the whispers: *Why does he get the praise while I do the dirty work? Why must I always be the villain?*

The Drawing on the Hearth

IT HAD BEEN A SHOCK to Cavan when he first discovered what the world truly thought of him—and how they imagined he looked. More than a shock, really. It was ridiculous... and deeply hurtful.

He knew that delivering coal instead of gifts wouldn't win him any popularity contests. But he had never imagined they feared and loathed him, as much as they apparently did.

The first time he saw himself through their eyes was on an otherwise ordinary Christmas Eve. Everything was going smoothly—in fact, he and Nicholas were even a little ahead of schedule. They had just reached Norway and were delivering to a row of snow-covered houses when something unusual caught Cavan's eye.

It was on the fireplace of a small grey stone cottage, right beside the treats that were left for Nicholas and the reindeer. A drawing, made with a lump of black charcoal, had been scrawled across the hearth. It showed a hideous creature: hunched back, twisted horns, one human foot and one animal-like hoof. Its hands were grotesque claws—drawn disproportionately large—and it was covered in fur that stuck up wildly in all directions. The drawing was inside a circle with a line through it, as if to fend off the creature.

Cavan stopped in his tracks, staring at the drawing in disbelief. His eyes widened. "How could anyone imagine such a terrible creature?"

Nicholas hesitated and then chuckled softly. "Yes, they got the likeness completely wrong, didn't they, old friend?" He gave Cavan a gentle pat on the shoulder.

"Wait—you know who this is supposed to be?" Cavan asked, his eyebrows raised.

"It's you, of course," Nicholas admitted, though his smile softened when he saw Cavan's expression. "But don't worry. They don't know you — not really. They've got it all wrong."

Cavan slowly stepped away from the fireplace, still staring at the charcoal drawing, half-expecting it to leap from the hearth and claw at him if he dared look away. His eyes caught his reflection in the polished brass trim—a glint of candlelight revealed his stunned expression. His hair was still neat, every dark wave in place. His face, though pale with shock, was still handsome—wasn't it?

How could they have gotten it so wrong? But of course, he knew. They feared him. They hated him.

He glanced at Nicholas, who was hoisting the big sack of toys over his shoulder. *It's all his fault.*

"Come on, let's keep moving so we stay ahead of schedule," said Nicholas cheerfully—utterly unaware of the storm quietly rising inside his oldest friend.

Ever since that Christmas Eve, Cavan had made a point of investigating the rumors people spread about him. The following December he decided to spy on the humans at their winter solstice celebrations. Cavan had heard that they gathered around huge bonfires and scared one another with stories of monsters and evil beings. If they thought of him as a beast like the picture on the fireplace showed, then he was bound to hear absurd, untrue stories about himself.

So, the day before the winter solstice celebrations began, Cavan made a quiet trip to a small village in Scandinavia. He told no one—not even his best friend, Nick—about his investigations.

He lurked in the shadows of their festive gatherings, listening and waiting to hear their awful tales.

Cavan spotted a middle-aged man with a long grey beard huddled around a fire with a group of children; this seemed like a good place to begin his eavesdropping.

"Not only does he deliver the coal, but he steals naughty children in the night and spanks them with twisted tree branches," the man said dramatically. The children gasped with horror. "But don't worry, you'll hear him coming," he continued, "because he's wrapped in chains and bells. You can hear him from a mile away."

"Yes, yes, I've heard the bells," one of the children called out.

That's just the jingling bells from your precious Father Christmas's smelly reindeer—or worse, the ridiculous bell dangling from the tip of his even more ridiculous hat, Cavan wanted to say out loud. Cavan on the other hand took pride in how quietly he could slip into the houses without being heard or seen. "Hear me coming from a mile away, utter nonsense," he scoffed.

"I'll just run away when I hear him," said another child.

"Ah, you must not know of his other power," the storyteller whispered. The children huddled closer to the fire and listened intently. "He can change shapes, he can be as small as a mouse, or as big as a house."

"They got that part right," Cavan muttered. He had that power along with his partner Nick. How else could they fit into small places like chimneys?

"And when he's as big as a house," the man stood up and stretched his arms out tall, his fingers curled like claws, "old Krampus will reach out and grab you, and there's no escape!" He suddenly lunged and tapped the nearest boy on the shoulder. The child jumped, and the others shrieked in delight.

The storyteller laughed a booming laugh, "come on," he said. "Let's find something to eat."

Cavan stood frozen in the shadows. "Krampus! Is that what they call me?"

Laughter, Cocoa, and Frost

CAVAN THREW OPEN THE living room door at the North Pole. Nick was standing in the middle of the room wearing a new half-sewn suit while Martha, his wife, moved around him, pinning and measuring.

"What's the matter?" she asked, looking up from her tape measure, immediately sensing that Cavan's mood was off.

"Krampus!" Cavan yelled. "Do you know that's what they call me? Krampus!"

"Oh, yes, I've heard them whispering that name," said Nicholas. He raised his hand, curling it into a playful claw.

Seeing Cavan's utterly bewildered look, he went on, "Krampus means claw." He made the claw again, this time adding a quiet growl and a chuckle. Martha nudged him. Nicholas quickly became serious when she gave him a stern warning look. "I'm sorry, old friend," he said.

Cavan looked down at his hands. His fingers were long and lean, his nails neatly trimmed.

"It's the coal handprints you're always leaving," said Nicholas interrupting his inspection. "I've told you time and again to be more careful. Those big hands of yours leave quite the mark—it's no wonder they think you have claws. Pay no attention to the silly stories."

"That's easy for you to say," Cavan shot back. "You've never been painted as a monster. Do you know how vile those tales are? They say I spank children! I shudder when I hear them, and I burn with anger too. How would you like it if the whole world whispered lies about you? It isn't right. It isn't fair. I care for the children of the world as much as you do — but they see me as a beast."

Martha placed her pin cushion and tape measure on the hearth and wrapped her arms around Cavan. "I hate that they say those things about you," she said softly. "But you know you're not the monster they imagine. If they really knew you—the real you—the stories would be so different."

Cavan nodded. Martha's soothing presence began to calm him. He could never stay angry for long when she was around. "I just don't think I can do it again this Christmas," he confessed. "Every year I go out there, the stories get worse—more twisted, and cruel."

"You're forgetting all of the good we do. And the laughs, don't forget the laughs," Nicholas said.

Cavan knew what was coming next. Nick was already grinning; he was about to tell one of his stories about some funny incident that happened to them during one of their deliveries. He couldn't be sure which one— there were so many of them.

"Do you remember that time I stumbled over a log by the fireplace and sent all of the knickknacks on the hearth flying?" said Nicholas, already in fits of laughter.

"Yes, and it made such a clatter," said Cavan. "You really are so noisy. It's a wonder you're not spotted more often."

"Then that man came to see what the noise was," Nicholas said between laughs, "and you just guided him back to bed."

"Told him he was still asleep, and it was all a dream," Cavan added proudly.

"And he believed you!" Nicholas turned to Martha, wiping away tears of laughter. "He just nodded, went back to bed, and never said a word." He turned back to Cavan, "you and that whisper of yours... you can talk anyone into anything."

A smile slowly started to appear on Cavan's lips. "Well, I wouldn't have to come up with such tricks if you'd be quieter."

The three of them laughed together, as they had a thousand times before.

"You can't give all of this up, old friend," said Nicholas as he gave Cavan a hearty pat on the back.

Feeling that the crisis had passed, Martha returned to her work. Cavan helped himself to some hot cocoa and leaned against the mantel, watching Martha adjust a seam on Nicholas's jacket.

Cavan had never understood Nick's fashion choices. He supposed the red suit must be warm enough for the frigid December deliveries—but red? Really?

Cavan preferred elegance. Styles changed, but he kept up — always refined, always effortless. He knew how to make an entrance without looking like a walking Christmas decoration.

On Christmas Eve, just before Cavan and Nicholas climbed into the sleigh, the trio gathered by the stables. Lantern light flickered across the snow, where the reindeer stamped impatiently.

Martha took each of them by the hand. "Keep safe," she said, giving both of their hands a gentle squeeze.

"Keep quiet," said Cavan, smirking at Nick.

"Keep believing," said Nicholas—then, with a booming laugh: "Ho, ho, ho! Merry Christmas!"

The trio had performed this ritual for years. Martha never let them leave the North Pole on Christmas Eve without these simple, meaningful gestures—a private tradition between just the three of them that prepared them for the long night ahead.

As the sleigh lifted into the sky, Martha watched until it disappeared beyond the clouds. She whispered a quiet prayer heavenwards and turned back towards her warm home, where she would be waiting for their safe return.

Once again, balance was restored—Nicholas, Martha and Cavan doing their important work together, a solid trio, supporting and caring for each other. But beneath the laughter and cocoa, cracks like frost on a windowpane had begun to spread. And no warmth, not even Martha's, could keep them from widening.

He's Checking It Twice

FOR A FEW YEARS, THE Christmas Eve deliveries went smoothly. Nicholas and Cavan moved in perfect rhythm—slipping down chimneys, leaving gifts and coal, bringing magic to the world.

But each song, each letter, each plate of treats for Father Christmas felt like a lump of his own coal dropping on Cavan's chest, until the weight smothered everything else. It was always for Nick, never for him.

Cavan became more distant from Martha and Nick. When they were together, he was all business. The laughter faded. The teasing stopped.

MARTHA SET HER FORK down with a soft clink. "I'm worried about Cavan," she said one evening as she and Nicholas sat down to dinner. "It's the fourth time I've invited him to eat with us, and every time he said he was busy. I think he's avoiding us."

Nicholas paused mid-bite, "I've been thinking the same thing," he admitted. "What do you think we should do?"

"I might write him a letter," she said quietly.

"That's a good idea." Nicholas gently patted her hand.

Cavan received twelve beautifully handwritten letters from Martha that year. She told him stories about the North Pole—updates from the workshop, new toy designs she was working on with the elves and funny things the reindeer had done. Every letter ended the same way: **Keep Safe. Keep Quiet. Keep Believing.**

Cavan stopped reading the letters after a while. Each one left him dangerously close to softening, and he couldn't afford softness anymore.

He never stopped lurking in the shadows, listening for stories about Krampus. The tales obsessed him. He memorized the worst ones. He let them fester.

Jealousy took hold of his soul. He began to wonder if Nick had planned it this way from the start—to be loved and adored, while Cavan became the one children feared. Cavan didn't want to be hated anymore. He wanted adoration. He wanted songs. Treats. Letters. Love.

These thoughts consumed him. What began as frustration hardened into bitterness. And bitterness, left unchecked, grew into something darker. Until one day, Cavan made a decision. He would no longer be the scary monster in the shadows, and if that meant turning Nick into the villain for once well, so be it.

*Let **him** see what it's like to be feared and loathed.*

*Let **him** see what it's like to be alone.*

Cavan spent weeks hatching up elaborate schemes, each one more complicated than the last. But one night, he jolted awake with a new idea—so simple, so perfect, he could hardly believe he hadn't thought of it before.

He would swap the Naughty and Nice lists—so the well-behaved children would wake to coal, and the naughty ones would be showered with gifts.

Nicholas always double-checked the Naughty and Nice list exactly one week before Christmas. "He's making a list and checking it twice" wasn't just a lyric—it was protocol. After Nick's final inspection, the list was sent to the workshop, where the elves began preparing the gifts—or the coal—and loading the sleigh.

All Cavan had to do was sneak into the workshop late one night and quietly switch the front covers of the two books—Nice labeled as Naughty, and Naughty labeled as Nice. Once the elves started their sorting, everything would fall perfectly into place.

When the children of the world woke to the wrong rewards on Christmas morning, it would be chaos. Parents would be upset—confused, maybe even furious. Cavan knew this act alone wouldn't bring down Nick entirely, but it was a good start.

"How could Father Christmas make such a mistake?" Cavan imagined them whispering. *"If he can't get this right, does he*

even care anymore?" And then perhaps he, Cavan, could be the one to swoop in and save the day.

He pictured himself calming the outrage, finding the solution, putting everything right again. Then they'd know who the real hero is.

When Cavan arrived at the North Pole to make the switch, he tried his best to act like his old self—warm, familiar, untroubled. No one could suspect a thing.

He even stopped by Martha's cozy living room, where the fireplace crackled and the room glowed with a thousand twinkling Christmas lights.

"Do you want to see some of the new toy designs we worked on this year?" Martha asked, her eyes shining with excitement.

"I'd love to," Cavan said with a warm smile.

Martha eagerly brought out drawings and blueprints, then prototypes—the sketches brought to life. Tiny wooden tops, soft-stitched dolls, clever little clockwork contraptions. All beautiful. All made with love.

"Martha designed most of them herself," said Nicholas, beaming. "Isn't she brilliant?"

Martha blushed. "It was a group effort," she said modestly.

"They're perfect," Cavan said quietly, quickly looking away from Martha. A pang of guilt struck. Doubt followed close behind.

Could he really go through with it? Let the children who hadn't earned a place on the nice list receive these toys—Martha's toys? It was clear that her heart was poured into every sketch, every stitch, every painted detail. And Martha's heart wasn't just any heart. It was gentle, and full of goodness.

The kind of goodness that made even the coldest places feel warm.

There was a time when Cavan believed no one knew him better than Martha. She had seen the best in him when no one else had bothered to look. Did she suspect what he was about to do? No. She was far too kind—too full of hope and trust—to imagine such betrayal. The thought wouldn't even enter her mind.

Cavan stole another glance at Martha, her face still glowing with excitement. He bent and brushed her cheek with a kiss — light, almost reverent. It was a farewell she could not recognize. Whatever followed his disloyalty, nothing between them would remain the same. The Cavan she knew was gone.

"I'd better get going. It's getting late," he said.

As he quietly closed the door behind him, he heard Martha say, "Oh Nick... he came back to us. It's just like old times."

Cavan stepped into the cold December night. The air was still and clear. Only the crunch of snow beneath his boots broke the silence.

At the workshop, the door creaked open. Inside, rows of benches stood silent, strewn with scraps of ribbon, wrapping paper, glitter, and tags. On the sorting table sat two thick books —one marked Nice, the other Naughty. One switch. That was all. One moment, and everything would change.

My Name is Krampus

SNOWFLAKES FELL SOFTLY on the North Pole stables as the three stood side by side: Nicholas, Martha, and Cavan—the trio who had shared laughter, tears, late nights, and long flights.

Cavan knew that things would never be the same after this delivery.

Would he miss the bonds, the love, the friendship? Certainly. Maybe all that was needed was this one reminder—a gentle nudge to Nick, that Cavan didn't always have to be the bad guy—and then things could go back to normal. But deep down, Cavan knew that wasn't true.

He glanced toward Martha. She stood nearby, chatting with one of the elves about some last-minute detail. Ever since

Cavan had returned last week, she'd been glowing—so sure that things were finally back to normal.

"Alright, looks like we're ready to go," Nicholas said, adjusting his gloves.

The three stepped into their familiar formation. Martha reached out and took Nicholas's hand in one of hers, and Cavan's in the other.

"Keep safe," she said softly, giving both hands a gentle squeeze.

"Keep quiet," Cavan replied, forcing a smile and avoiding their eyes.

"Keep believing!" boomed Nicholas into the starry sky.

As the sleigh prepared for takeoff, Martha called after them, "I love you both! I have a feeling this will be one of our best Christmas Eves ever!"

Cavan closed his eyes.

At first, watching the wrong gifts go to the wrong children made Cavan's stomach tight and queasy. But then he began to see the usual notes and treats lovingly left for Father Christmas. They adored him more than ever. Cavan reassured himself. This had to be done. It was the only way to fix things.

As the night wore on, he grew more cheerful—almost giddy. A few times, he even tossed in extra pieces of coal for the "naughty" children. This made him laugh out loud.

When they returned to the North Pole, Cavan quickly excused himself and slipped away, eager to spy on the fallout. He had long since mastered his gift for changing form. He could shrink small enough to slip through keyholes and window cracks, or become a wisp of cloud, invisible to all. These gifts were perfect for plotting, spying, and scheming.

Cavan slipped into a cozy-looking home with a holly wreath on the front door. It seemed a good place to start observing the mayhem. Inside, a child who certainly belonged on the naughty list squealed with delight as he unwrapped a beautifully wrapped toy. His parents looked at each other in stunned disbelief. They had warned him all year that if his behavior didn't improve, Krampus would bring him a lump of coal.

"Bet you don't think old Krampus is so bad now, do you?" Cavan whispered into the boy's ear, his voice barely more than vapor.

"I like Krampus. He's not so bad," the boy said aloud. His parents stared at him, more shocked than ever.

"It's working," Cavan whispered to himself. "My plan is working."

He moved on to the next house. There, a girl who had *always* been on the good list sat in silence, tears streaming down her cheeks as she stared at a lump of coal in her hands. Her parents sat on either side, patting her back, whispering reassurances.

The sight made Cavan's chest ache with remorse. This wasn't what he'd wanted. It had all begun with the hope of making every child happy — even the ones who hadn't quite earned it. But that flicker of regret soured as he heard the mother whisper, "I think this is all Krampus's fault."

Cavan's stomach twisted. *No,* he wanted to scream. *It's not my fault. Well... technically, it is—but you're supposed to blame Nick, not me.* House after house told the same story.

"Krampus," they cried. "Krampus did this. Father Christmas could never be so cruel."

Cavan was devastated. Worse still, the stories about him were getting darker and stranger. "He has mindless minions, thousands of them, who obey his every wicked command," a teenage boy whispered to a group of younger children. "Father Christmas has elves. Krampus has ugly minions who hide in the shadows and spy on you." The boy scrunched his face to look monstrous. The rest of the children squealed.

Cavan fled. He didn't know where to go, or what to do. He felt utterly beaten down. He had never felt so unhappy—or hopeless. Maybe they were right. Maybe he was evil. After all, he had betrayed his best friends. He decided to return to the North Pole. He wasn't sure whether he was returning to confess or gloat. Either way he was ready to face the music.

Inside the main hall, Nicholas and Martha were seated at the long table alongside several senior elves. An emergency meeting was underway. Word of the delivery disaster had already reached them.

"I just don't know how it happened," said Horace, the head elf. "I take full responsibility."

"It was me," Cavan said quietly, still standing in the doorway.

The room fell silent. All eyes turned to him.

"Well, then I'm sure it was just an accident," Martha said quickly. "We'll find a way to fix it. Don't you worry or feel bad." She smiled gently.

"It wasn't an accident," Cavan replied. "I deliberately did it."

For a moment the crackling fire was the only sound in the room.

"Is this about all the Krampus nonsense?" Nicholas asked, rubbing his forehead. "Because we've been over this again and again. It's ludicrous, old friend. Pay no attention."

Why does Nick never take me seriously? Why does he always brush it off?

He felt rage boiling up inside of him until he could contain it no longer. Cavan clenched his fists. His nails lengthened. His shoulders hunched forward, his spine cracking with each movement. No one spoke. And then, with a growl that shook the room, he was Krampus.

The man who once prided himself on elegance and poise had become the nightmare from the hearth drawing — twisted horns, hunched shoulders, claws instead of hands.

"If it is a monster they want," he roared, "then that is what they shall have!"

"They got the story wrong," Martha said, rising to her feet. "That doesn't mean you have to live it."

"It's over. I'm leaving," Cavan hissed.

"Please, don't go. Let's talk and work this out," Martha pleaded.

"Yes, please, Cavan," Nicholas said softly. A single tear rolled down his cheek. "Let's talk."

Cavan turned to the door. "Don't call me Cavan." He looked back once more; his eyes filled with fury and grief. "My name is Krampus."

The Monster They Made

KRAMPUS NEVER RETURNED to his true form—never became Cavan again. For decades, he listened to the tales that were told about him: evil, hideous, heartless. The words echoed until they took root. In time, he began to believe them—becoming the very creature they feared, living out every trait and terror they had whispered in their stories. Sometimes, it's hard to remember who you really are when everyone else has already decided for you.

Martha never stopped sending him letters, pleading for him to come back. He never opened them, yet he couldn't bring himself to throw them away. Instead, he tucked each one carefully aside, the stack growing year after year. Each letter stirred within him the pain of losing Martha — the pain he tried so hard to bury and keep hidden.

The jealousy and bitterness he felt toward Nicholas slowly hardened into hate. And that hatred soon spread to the things Nicholas loved most—everything except Martha. Never Martha. But Christmas itself he despised; he couldn't bear its light, not when he felt such darkness within himself.

So, he did what he could to ruin it. All year long, Krampus schemed with his "minions"—though in truth, they were nothing more than smoky illusions, extensions of himself with no minds of their own. Just another part of the story he'd made real.

When December came each year, his plans would become reality. He soared across the globe in his smoky Krampus form, sowing mischief wherever he went. It was easy to twist the humans' joyful preparations into stress and exhaustion.

At parties, he whispered poisonous thoughts that sparked arguments. When children wrote their Christmas lists, he nudged them toward greed. Whatever joy he couldn't destroy outright, he soured at the edges. Mischief was the only thing that seemed to make him happy—or so he told himself. For no one can be truly happy while making others miserable.

He tried to avoid Nicholas whenever he could. The man's relentless joy and cheer made him feel weak and sick to his core. But since both of them worked in the same business—Christmas—it was inevitable that their paths would cross from time to time.

Every time they did, it was the same: *"We love you. Come back to us. Making others miserable won't make you feel better."*

One Christmas Eve—at a time and place far removed from the centuries he'd spent with Nick and Martha—Krampus and Nicholas unexpectedly crossed paths again.

For a few years now, Krampus had set his sights on causing misery for one family in particular: the Christmas family. Their name dated back hundreds of years, given to them because they organized the most joyous Christmas celebrations. Nicholas had known—and loved—the Christmas family for generations. If Krampus could sour their sickly-sweet Christmas spirit, he would have accomplished something truly remarkable. Breaking the Christmas family's hope and spirit was the first step to unraveling Nick's world.

Cunning old Krampus waited until he thought Nick had finished his deliveries to the family's home in the quaint little village of Windlesham in England. Only then did he slip through the cracks in their front door and slink toward the living room, ready to unleash his mischief.

But what he saw stopped him cold. There, kneeling beside the tree, pulling presents from his sack, was the jolly fat man himself. Had Nick deliberately tricked him so he could try to stop him or lecture him? "Probably," hissed Krampus.

"Hello there, my old friend," said Nicholas without even looking up, as if he'd been expecting him. "What brings you here tonight?"

"You know very well why I'm here... Santa or whatever ridiculous name you're going by these days," he answered, his voice full of disdain.

"Why don't you tell me what's bothering you? Perhaps we can talk things through," Nick said, his voice as warm as ever.

Krampus sarcastically mimicked, "'Why don't you tell me what's bothering you.' Oh, you'd love that, wouldn't you? Maybe you'd like me to lie on the couch and spill all my problems."

Nicholas smiled, unfazed. "If that would make you more comfortable."

"Why don't you mind your own business for once and stop trying to fix me," Krampus snapped.

"Alright," Nicholas said calmly, still placing presents under the tree.

Nicholas's laid- back attitude irritated Krampus more than his meddling. "That's it? No lectures this time? No, *'leave the poor Christmas family alone, Krampus. Don't spread your misery, Krampus'*—blah, blah, blah?"

Nicholas let out a deep, jolly laugh. "I see you've been listening all these years. But no, no lectures tonight."

"Why not? Too busy delivering your hideous presents?" Krampus jeered.

"I'm never too busy for you, old friend."

"Then why hold back? Where's the annoying moralizing?"

"You'll do what you do, no matter what I say. But go ahead, I'm not worried," Nicholas replied.

Krampus scowled. "You're treating me like an amateur. We've known each other for centuries—you know what I'm capable of."

"I do. But I also know what **they're** capable of. Yes, you can stir up some trouble, but you can't break their Christmas spirit or the love they have for each other." Nicholas spoke with conviction.

Krampus folded his arms and huffed. "We'll see about that. Now get out of here so I can get to work."

"As you wish. Forgive me," Nicholas said as he slung his sack over his shoulder and moved to the fireplace.

What's he up to? Krampus's jaw tightened. *Trying to unnerve me? Or does he really think I can't do it?*

"Good night, old friend. Merry Christmas! Let's catch up sometime, grab some lunch," Nicholas said brightly. With a whoosh, he shot up the chimney.

"'Let's catch up, grab some lunch,'" Krampus again mimicked. "When will the old fool accept, we're not best pals anymore? Those days are long gone," he hissed.

Krampus grimaced at the sound of reindeer hooves on the roof and the jingle of sleigh bells. "Ho, ho, ho! Merry Christmas!" echoed Nicholas's voice down the chimney.

Shiny Awards

AS SOON AS NICHOLAS returned to the North Pole, he hurried to Martha and told her about his encounter with Cavan.

"He's set his sights on Hector Christmas—the youngest son. Cavan's plotting some scheme to turn the family against him," Nicholas said, tugging off his gloves.

"Oh, Nick, how dreadful. Why does he do these things?"

Nicholas tossed a log onto the fire. "He's bitter, and misery loves company. But he won't break the Christmas family's spirit."

"I hope you're right," Martha murmured. "It's families like theirs that keep the spirit of Christmas alive."

Nicholas nodded, though his eyes were troubled. "The problem is, Cavan doesn't give up easily. Every defeat only drives him to scheme bigger."

"What can we do to stop him?" Martha asked.

"We can't stop him. But we can keep watch. I'll have our chaps keep an eye on the Christmas family. And you know, as well as I do, that others will be paying close attention." He reached across and patted her hand. "Now, speaking of the Christmas family, I still need to finish Holly's birthday present."

Holly was the youngest of the Christmas children, and her birthday was on Christmas Day. Years ago, Nicholas had made a special arrangement with her father, John, to deliver her birthday presents each year at exactly 2:00 p.m.—the time she was born.

"Imagine that—a baby born to the Christmas family on Christmas Day," John had said in awe when he excitedly called Nicholas to share the news.

A smile returned to Martha's face. "How old is Holly now?"

"She's ten years old," said Nicholas proudly.

WINTER PASSED, AND soon green shoots of daffodils began to push through the damp ground. Nicholas hadn't stopped worrying about Cavan and what he might be scheming.

One afternoon, a quiet knock came at his office door.

"Come in," Nicholas called.

"Sorry to bother you," Horace said, slipping inside and quietly closing the door behind him.

"No bother at all," Nicholas replied with a warm smile. "What can I do for you today?"

"You said to keep an eye on the Christmas family."

Nicholas nodded.

"I've got some news about John Christmas." Horace stepped forward to Nicholas's desk.

"Oh?" Nicholas looked up, over his glasses. "Please, have a seat. What's going on?"

Horace sat down. "John Christmas was given the *Mayor's Outstanding Citizen Award*—for a donation to his local library. It was on the news. Probably nothing. If anything, it's good press for John, but I thought you should know."

"Hmmm..." Nicholas tapped a pen thoughtfully against the desk. "There's something fishy about this. John goes to great lengths to keep all of his charitable giving quiet. Somebody must've tipped off the mayor's office – or the press. What's he up to?" Nicholas wondered aloud.

"Who? John?" Horace asked.

"No, not John. Cavan," Nicholas said, still tapping the pen lightly.

"Krampus? What would he have to do with it?" Horace blinked, confused. "If anything, it's been very quiet on that front. No sightings of him or .... his creatures since last Christmas."

Nicholas leaned back in his chair. "Quiet doesn't mean idle." His eyes narrowed in thought. "He's laying the groundwork, I'd wager."

Then, slowly, a look of realization crossed Nicholas's face. "The higher the rise, the greater the fall," he said quietly.

KRAMPUS PERCHED HIGH in the rafters of the town hall, his crooked, gnarled legs dangling and swinging like a happy child. The hall was empty now, except for the janitor, who slowly pushed his mop back and forth across the floor. Only hours earlier, it had been crowded with happy do-gooders, clapping families, and shiny awards.

The plaques had already been nailed to the wall for everyone to see. And there in the center hung John's: **Outstanding Citizen, 1959 — John Christmas.**

After his miserable failure last Christmas with Hector, Krampus had slunk back to the solace of his icy cavern. He ranted and raved to his 'minions' for hours, and then suddenly a thought came to him: he'd been going about things all wrong, aiming at the wrong target. To unravel the whole family, he needed to topple their pillar — John Christmas. "That man and his relentless cheer, he's almost as bad as Nick," he hissed.

He slipped down from the beam and glided across the polished floor, his shadow stretching long and thin behind him. With a crooked claw, he tapped the brass plate of John's plaque.

"Outstanding, indeed," he muttered. "Ah, but nothing stays shiny forever, does it? Sooner or later, someone asks the wrong questions, someone looks too closely. Rise high, John Christmas. Your fall is coming, and it will be a sight to behold." With a delighted snicker, he melted back into the dark.

We're All Family Here

"I'M SNEAKING OUT FOR a couple of hours," said John Christmas, poking his head around the doorway of his office manager, Jane Pengilly.

John was always an upbeat, cheerful fellow, but she could tell something had gotten him especially giddy today.

"What are you so happy about?" Jane looked up from the papers strewn across her desk.

John's eyes lit up with excitement. "It's a secret," he said with a wink.

Jane raised an eyebrow. "Hmm... very mysterious. Well, I'll let you be on your way. Oh, but—wait a minute." She stopped him as he reached for the door. "The new accountant is coming today."

John hesitated.

"Go, go." Jane waved him off with a small smile. "I'll deal with it."

"You're a lifesaver!" John called as he dashed out of the door.

Jane let out a weary sigh and pushed the papers on her desk into a neater pile. *Well, this lot won't sort itself out.*

John was on his way to special-order a new twenty-three-inch television, housed in a beautiful oak console. *Twenty-three inches!* he thought in wonder as he hurried to catch the Tube. *What will they think of next?*

In just a few months, the world would welcome a new decade—1960! John could already feel the buzz of it. He loved the thrill of modern invention: sleek motorcars, transistor radios, automatic toasters. The future, he thought, looked dazzling. And what better way to welcome it than with a brand-new, state-of-the-art television set?

Mary would scold him, of course, calling it too extravagant. But John smiled to himself. The importing business, passed down through the Christmas family for generations, had treated him well. Surely there was no harm in celebrating the future with a little extravagance.

While John bustled off towards Harrods electrical department, Jane welcomed the new accountant to Christmas Imports. A tall, well-dressed man stepped into her office with a charming smile and an outstretched hand.

"Hello. Bryan Higgin. I believe you're expecting me," he said.

"Hello," Jane said, rising to shake his hand. "Nice to see you again. How was your trip in?"

"Smooth as could be," Bryan replied. "I even found a little café nearby that serves the most delicious custard tarts. I think I'm going to like it here."

"I'm glad to hear it," Jane said with a friendly smile. "Well then, shall we? I'll show you around and take you to your office."

"Lead the way," Bryan said cheerfully.

As Bryan followed Jane out of her office she continued, "Mr. Christmas sends his apologies for not being here. He stepped out for a bit." She lowered her voice. "I don't know exactly what he's up to. He says it's a secret."

"Hmm, sounds interesting," said Bryan, raising an eyebrow.

The main office floor stretched out in a long, orderly room where desks stood in tidy rows. Each workstation bore small signs of life: mugs with fading lipstick prints, biscuit tins shared between desk-mates, and framed photographs of loved ones — smiling in front of caravans, windswept on seaside holidays, or gathered around Christmas trees.

The steady clack of typewriters filled the room, underscored by the gentle hum of conversation and the occasional burst of laughter.

"This is where it all happens," said Jane proudly.

"So, I see," Bryan replied, glancing around. "I don't think I've ever seen such a cheerful office. Most places I've worked, people keep their heads down and mind their own business. Mr. Christmas must be working some kind of magic."

Jane smiled with a small nod.

"Now let's get you to your office," she said, leading the way.

She opened a door off the main office floor to reveal a small, comfortable room. On the desk sat a well-used adding machine, its paper roll curled from the last sum, and a black leather-bound ledger. A pot of fresh flowers stood on the window ledge.

"I hope you'll be comfortable here," Jane said, giving the room a once-over.

"It's lovely, Miss Pengilly, but..." Bryan hesitated, glancing toward the door.

"Go on, Mr. Higgin," she encouraged kindly.

"Well... I hate to be difficult, but I wonder—do you have something a bit more tucked away? It's just that I tend to get distracted when there's too much going on around me. I work best with as few interruptions as possible."

"Oh," Jane said, blinking. "Well, we do have another space, further from the main office floor. But it hasn't been used in years. I'm not sure it's even in suitable condition."

"I don't need anything fancy," Bryan said with an easy smile. "Just a desk and a chair. I'd be ever so grateful."

"Well," said Jane, already heading for the door, "let's go have a look and see what we can make of it."

Jane unlocked a narrow wooden door at the far end of the corridor. A musty, dusty odor hit them as soon as the door creaked open. "It's freezing in here," she said, as she stepped inside. The air felt damp and stale, like it hadn't been disturbed in years.

She crossed the small, windowless space and switched on a lamp. It sputtered to life with a flicker and a buzz, casting a weak glow that barely reached the edges of the room. Long shadows stretched across the paint-chipped concrete walls, where spiderwebs clung in the corners. A worn desk stood in the center, its surface coated in a thick layer of dust. An old chair with cracked leather leaned slightly to one side.

Jane coughed gently into her sleeve and brushed dust from the chair's backrest. "We can't have you working in here, Mr. Higgin."

Bryan stepped further inside, his eyes calmly taking in the heavy door, the concrete walls and the distant hum of the office far behind them. "It's perfect, Miss Pengilly. I promise," he said cheerfully, his tone warm and unbothered.

"Well, let me at least have an electric heater sent over for you. And a new lamp," Jane said, eyeing the still-flickering bulb with concern.

"No, no. I prefer it on the cooler side. And I'll fiddle with the lamp—see if I can fix it. It's got character," he added with a small chuckle.

Jane hesitated, rubbing her arms against the chill. "It doesn't seem right to leave you in here. If you change your mind, you be sure to let me know," she said, with one more worried glance around the room. "Let's go back to my office. I've got some paperwork for you to make everything official."

"Do you have family nearby, Miss Pengilly?" Bryan asked politely as they walked back through the hallway and onto the bustling main floor.

Jane paused. "No, not really. I did once... I was engaged, years ago. But Trevor passed away before we could set a date."

Bryan's expression softened. "I'm sorry to hear that."

"Thank you. He was a good man." She looked down at her shoes, then straightened with quiet pride. "But I've got my family right here. Birthdays, Christmas parties—cake for any excuse."

"I'll have to start remembering birthdays, then," Bryan said with a chuckle. "I can already tell you take care of everyone here, Miss Pengilly. The glue that holds it all together."

"Perhaps," she said modestly.

As Jane pulled forms from a filing cabinet, a young secretary appeared at Jane's office door with a polite knock.

"Excuse me, Miss Pengilly. I was told to bring these to you for Mr. Christmas to sign."

"Oh, thank you, Pam," Jane said, accepting the stack of papers. "How are you settling in?"

"Very well, thank you."

Jane gestured toward Pam. "Mr. Higgin, this is Pam. She started last week."

Bryan rose effortlessly from his chair and extended his hand. "Hello," he said warmly. "I'm Bryan Higgin."

"Hello," Pam stammered, shaking his hand. With his blond hair and dazzling smile, he looked like a film star stepped straight off the cinema screen. But what truly took her breath away were his eyes. Even behind his glasses, they were stunning — a piercing, icy blue, unlike any she had ever seen.

As Pam and Bryan exchanged greetings, Jane flipped through the papers before glancing up apologetically. "Forgive me, Mr. Higgin — this will just take a minute."

"It's quite all right," Bryan replied smoothly, gathering the papers Jane handed him. "Why don't I take these back to my office and get started? I'll let you know if I have any questions." He paused, his gaze flicking briefly to Pam before returning to

Jane. Pam's heart pounded as his icy blue eyes found hers again — just for a moment.

"And please," he added with a smile, "call me Bryan. As you said earlier, we're all family here."

Custard Tarts and Walks in the Park

BRYAN HAD QUICKLY EARNED his way into the hearts of the employees at Christmas Imports — especially the young, single secretaries. But it seemed he only had eyes for Pam, the shy, soft-spoken newcomer.

Every morning at precisely 10:00 a.m., Bryan and Pam took their mid-morning break together.

The tradition began the day after Bryan started at Christmas Imports. Bryan had bumped into Pam in the break room. "Hello again," he said with a bright smile. "Remember me? We met yesterday in Miss Pengilly's office."

Remember you? Pam thought. *How could I forget?* "Yes, of course," she said aloud, trying to sound composed. "Nice to see you again."

She opened her handbag and pulled out a few snacks.

"You're more organized than I am," Bryan laughed. "I didn't bring a thing. Can't stop thinking about the custard tart from that café down the road, though."

Pam laughed nervously. She didn't know how to talk to someone like him—so confident, so handsome.

"Hey, Pam," Bryan said, lowering his voice just a little. "I have an idea. Let's sneak out and grab one of those custard tarts. My treat. Us newbies need to stick together," he added with a chuckle.

"Oh... um... I—" Pam could barely string a sentence together, let alone imagine walking to the café and sitting with him. She simply nodded.

"Settling in alright, Mr. Higgin?" Pam asked timidly, wrapping her hands around her warm mug as they sat across from each other in the cozy café.

Bryan gave a crooked grin. "Oh, call me Bryan, please. 'Mr. Higgin' makes me sound like a grumpy old headmaster."

"Alright, Bryan. How's it going then? Feeling at home yet? How's your office?"

Bryan whispered in a dramatic tone, "I think my office is haunted." Pam's eyes widened. "The radiator is stone cold, completely dead, but every so often it lets out a groan, like something's trapped inside. And my lamp flickers like it's possessed."

Pam giggled. "Well, you'd better keep an eye out for ghostly pens flying at your head."

Bryan nodded with a chuckle. He took a slow sip of his drink, then added lightly, "Have you seen Mr Christmas's office? It's stunning—big windows, a great view of the city." He leaned in closer to Pam. "But enough about work. Tell me more about you."

"Oh, there's not much to tell, really," Pam said, her eyes dropping to her mug. "I'm not very interesting, I'm afraid."

"Nonsense," said Bryan smoothly. "I don't believe that for a second. What do you do when you're not keeping things running at Christmas Imports?"

"Well... it's silly, really." She looked away and tucked a loose strand of hair behind her ear.

"Come on, Pam. You can trust me," he said softly, his tone warm and reassuring.

She hesitated, then gave a shy smile. "I like to write. I used to write for the school newspaper."

"Really? What kind of things do you write about?" Bryan asked, clearly intrigued.

"This is the part you'll think is silly. I like writing children's stories—especially ones about Christmas. I just... I've always loved Christmas." Her face lit up.

Bryan's smile widened. "Christmas stories, huh? That's... really lovely." He glanced toward the window, where the sun was just starting to break through the clouds. "We should probably head back. What do you say to a walk back through the park?"

So began the first of many custard tarts and park strolls for Bryan and Pam. Over the long summer, Bryan made himself part of Pam's world. He listened to her stories about her family and made her laugh with his jokes and impressions of the others at the office. Their 10 o'clock break together quickly became the best part of Pam's day.

One morning, as they walked back through the park, Bryan's eyes twinkled with mischief.

"As I was leaving to meet you," he began, "June—the tea lady—was rolling her trolley across the office floor..." He suddenly straightened his back, pushed an imaginary cart in front of him, and in a singsong voice called, "Tea, luv? Two sugars?"

Pam clapped a hand over her mouth, trying not to laugh too loudly. "Oh, stop it! You sound just like her!"

Bryan winked and added, "Mind the wheels, dear, they've got a mind of their own." He gave the trolley an exaggerated shove, nearly stumbling for effect.

The leaves in the park were just beginning to change colors, making the world glow with the warmth of orange and yellow. For the first time since joining Christmas Imports, Pam felt as though she truly belonged—and Bryan was the reason.

But while Pam's world grew more comfortable and content, far away another festered in cold and misery.

LATE ONE EVENING, KRAMPUS stalked the length of his icy cavern. Smoke from his "minions" curled and whispered at his feet as he muttered to them, his voice rising into sudden outbursts. Claws scraped stone as he flung his arms wide. Most of the words blurred into snarls—except for one name that rang out again and again:

"Bryan!"

At last, he halted, chest heaving, eyes blazing. "That fool... I thought I could use him. But he's growing soft. Distracted by the girl." His lips peeled back in a jagged grin. "It's time I took back control."

The Finest in London

A FEW MONTHS LATER, on a crisp December morning, Mary Christmas stepped off the train at Waterloo Station into the bustle of London. She was on her way to John's office—Christmas shopping and lunch awaited. Mary rarely came to the city, but every December she made certain of at least one visit.

She **loved** the city in December: the festive shop windows dressed with tinsel and toys; the towering Christmas trees strung with twinkling lights. In the foggy air, each bulb seemed to glow with its own halo. She inhaled deeply, catching the scent of roasted chestnuts from the street vendors on nearly every corner. London was always remarkable to Mary, but London at Christmastime was truly magical.

When she arrived at Christmas Imports, Mary didn't go straight to John's office. Her first stop was Jane's. Mary adored Jane—and the feeling seemed mutual.

Jane sprang up from her desk and hugged her tightly. "It's been too long, Mary! Tell me everything—what's new with you and the family?"

Mary laughed. "Well, that's a tall order. Where to begin?"

"Oh, I heard that John brought home an expensive new television. What did everyone think?" Jane asked, her eyes narrowed with curiosity.

"That's a good place to start," Mary replied with a chuckle. "I'm sure you heard how excited John was."

Jane nodded.

Mary went on, "So everyone's watching him set it up, and the whole time he's saying, *'Wait until you see the picture—you'll be amazed. The screen's so big it'll feel like the people are in your living room.'* Then, when it's finally on, Holly leans over to me and whispers, *'The picture doesn't look any different from the old television.'* And I whisper back, *'Don't tell your dad—he'll be furious.'*"

Jane rolled her eyes. "Oh yes, best not to criticize his beloved television."

At that moment, Jane glanced up and saw Bryan standing in the doorway.

"I'm sorry to interrupt, ladies," he said politely.

"Oh, Bryan! Come in, come in. Have you met Mary Christmas— John's wife?" Jane said, gesturing toward Mary.

"I don't believe I have," Bryan replied with an easy smile, stepping forward and extending his hand. "How do you do?"

"Very well, thank you. Lovely to meet you, Bryan. I've heard lots of nice things about you," Mary said as she shook his hand.

Their eyes met for a moment too long. *I know him from somewhere... don't I?* The thought came sharp and sudden, but the memory slipped away before she could grasp it. With looks like his, she should have remembered. And yet something in those piercing pale blue eyes made her skin prickle — as though they belonged to a place she would rather not revisit.

Bryan stood perfectly still, his smile tightening by a fraction. His grip was cool, and for the briefest moment, she thought she saw a flicker of shadow cross his face.

Mary broke the handshake and stepped back. "I'm here to meet John for lunch," she said quickly.

Just then, John popped his head around the door. "And you still won't tell me where you want to go," he teased.

"I told you, John — fish and chips on a bench in Trafalgar Square will do just fine. We don't need anywhere fancy."

"Nonsense," said John. "It's not every day my best girl comes to the city. I'm taking you to the finest restaurant in London. But first, some Christmas shopping at Harrods!" He rubbed his hands together, his face brimming with excitement.

Mary glanced back at Bryan. His cool gaze lingered on her and John. How could such a handsome face carry something so... off? The feeling clung to her like the chill of his handshake, urging her to leave.

"Have a great time, you two," Jane called as they went.

Bryan watched them walk out of the door. "How nice," he said lightly. "Mr. Christmas certainly knows how to enjoy the season. New televisions, shopping at Harrods, expensive lunches in the city..."

Jane nodded. "So, Bryan, what can I help you with?" she asked.

"I just stopped by to drop off a little Christmas gift," he said modestly. "Just a small token of appreciation, for all that you do around here." He placed a festive tin of biscuits on her desk.

"That's so thoughtful of you! Thank you, Bryan. You always think of others—no wonder everyone's so fond of you." She reached for the lid. "Shall we sneak one now?" she asked with a cheeky grin.

PAM AND BRYAN SAT TOGETHER at their usual table in the café. Even though Pam felt more comfortable around him now, her heart still quickened every time he smiled at her.

"So, what's the news from the main floor?" Bryan asked, taking the last bite of his custard tart.

"Well, Frank's wife had her baby," Pam said, beaming.

"Yes, yes—I heard! I was over there this morning to see Miss Pengilly. I told Frank he'd better bring in photographs soon," Bryan said with enthusiasm.

Pam nodded, smiling into her mug.

"I met Mrs. Christmas while I was in Jane's office," Bryan said lightly, stirring his drink. "She and Mr. Christmas rushed off to Harrods for Christmas shopping and then to some fancy restaurant for lunch."

Around them, spoons clinked against mugs, and from the wireless behind the counter came the smooth voice of Nat King Cole singing *When I Fall in Love*. Pam wondered if he noticed the song.

Bryan smiled again. "Us ordinary folk are happy with a simple custard tart, eh, Pam?" he said with a wink.

Pam blushed. She never felt ordinary when Bryan looked at her like that. "I look forward to my custard tart every day. And our chats, of course."

"Me too," Bryan said, grinning. "Hey, how was the surprise party for your parents' anniversary last night?"

They continued their cozy chat, not noticing the raindrops tapping against the café window as a drizzle began to fall.

A LITTLE LATER, ACROSS the city, John and Mary sat facing each other in an elegant restaurant, a harpist played softly in the corner. Outside, the rain picked up, drumming harder on the windowpanes, nearly drowning out the music.

"I think a storm's coming," John said, setting his crystal glass gently on the white linen tablecloth.

The temperature in the restaurant seemed to drop. Daylight dimmed as clouds rolled heavy and dark across the London sky. Thunder cracked overhead, making the silverware rattle faintly against the plates.

Mary shivered.

Numbers Don't Lie

EARLY ONE MORNING IN the middle of December, Bryan knocked on Jane's office door.

"Come in," Jane called. "Hello, Bryan," she added, looking up from her desk. "What can I do for you?"

"I just have a couple of questions. Mind if I sit? This might take a few minutes," Bryan asked, already pulling out a chair.

"Of course. Happy to help in any way I can," Jane said brightly.

Bryan took a seat and placed the company's ledger on Jane's desk. "I've been reviewing some of the company's financial records for the end of the year," he said casually, "and I noticed a number of inconsistencies—some fairly large cash withdrawals with no corresponding paperwork. I thought I'd check with you before bothering Mr. Christmas. Figured if anyone had the inside scoop, it'd be you."

"Oh?" Jane leaned in, curious.

"Here, for example," Bryan said, pointing to a highlighted line in the ledger. "May 1959—one thousand pounds withdrawn. But there's no receipt, no memo, no invoice. And there are a number of others like it throughout the year."

Jane studied the figures, then looked back up at Bryan. "It's... nothing to worry about."

"Nothing to worry about?" Bryan repeated. "But we do need to account for these expenditures."

Jane's gaze drifted out onto the office floor. "There are just some things Mr. Christmas prefers to keep quiet about his spending," she said, her voice quieter now.

"But I have to categorize this money somehow."

"Put it under charitable giving," Jane replied quickly, glancing out at the office floor again.

"Charitable giving?" he echoed. "With no proof, how can you be certain it's charitable giving?" Bryan's voice was barely above a whisper.

Jane didn't respond. She felt confused — not certain of anything.

Bryan smiled — a warm, almost reassuring smile. "It seems there's more to John Christmas than meets the eye." His tone was mild, but something in it made the hairs rise on the back of her neck. His gaze locked on hers — those icy blue eyes seemed to look straight through her. Jane quickly looked away. There was something unsettling about the way he watched her, as if willing her to speak — to say things she shouldn't.

She blinked hard and tore her gaze free. "I'm really not supposed to talk about this," she said, her voice unsteady. "So, if that's all, Bryan, I've got plenty to finish myself before the end of the year." She forced a thin, professional smile.

She'd never seen this side of Bryan before. Usually, he was easygoing, friendly — even charming. But now the warmth was gone, replaced by something cold and insistent. A chill crept through the room, and Jane rubbed her arms against it.

Bryan nodded slowly and shut the ledger. "Thank you for your help," he said flatly, though his voice lingered in her mind long after he'd left — as if he'd whispered something she couldn't quite remember.

Jane leaned back in her chair, exhaling a shaky breath. She hoped he'd let the matter drop, but something told her he wouldn't. John would not be happy with the questions. She'd covered for his secret spending before, but it never got easier. How long could she keep this up? Secrets had a way of surfacing — and now, she wasn't sure whose voice was telling her that.

THAT MORNING, AT THE café, Pam could tell something was off with Bryan.

"You alright?" she asked. "You've hardly touched your custard tart. You're usually done before I've had two bites."

Bryan smiled weakly. "I suppose I'm not much company today."

"What's wrong?" Pam asked, leaning in.

He sighed and rubbed his temples. "I hate to drag you into this, Pam."

"Please," she said, "let me help."

"I had a talk with Jane this morning. About the books," he said with a weary smile.

"The books?" Pam asked, puzzled.

Bryan lowered his voice. "The company's books. Large sums of money are gone with no explanation. When I asked Jane about it, she brushed it off—called it 'charitable giving.'" He shook his head slowly. "But she wouldn't look me in the eye. Kept glancing at the door, like she was afraid someone might overhear.

"I don't understand," Pam said. "John Christmas owns the company — technically he can do what he wants with the money. Why would Jane be afraid to tell you what's going on?"

"That's what's niggling at me. If it's all above board, why the whispers and the secrecy?"

Pam's eyes widened. She glanced nervously around the café. "What are you going to do?"

He shook his head. "I don't know. Everything else in this company runs like clockwork — all the i's dotted, all the t's crossed. The finances are meticulous too, except for several large, unaccounted-for expenses each year. It just doesn't make sense."

Bryan looked at Pam, waiting for a reaction. She sat quiet and wide-eyed. "I've even gone back a few years and checked the previous years' books," he added. They're all the same. Every year, money missing and no explanation."

He paused, tracing the rim of his cup. "Maybe... would you take a look at the books? Just to see if I've missed something. If there's an innocent explanation I'm not seeing?"

Pam nodded and tucked a loose strand of hair behind her ear. "I'm no accountant like you," she said gently, "but if it would help, of course I'll take a look."

"Thank you, Pam. I don't usually like being wrong—but in this case, I hope more than anything that I am."

LATE THAT EVENING, Krampus slipped through the crack beneath Bryan's office door. "Cozy," he snickered, surveying the dark, damp, windowless room. The company ledger lay in the center of the desk. With a frosty breath he stirred its edges, coaxing hidden slips of paper to jut out — just enough to catch the eye.

"Wait until the girl finds these little treasures," he murmured with a low chuckle.

He smiled at the bleak little room one last time before pulling the heavy door open. The hinges groaned. His twisted claw lingered on the handle as he left it slightly ajar.

"You can't hide behind ledgers and smiles forever, John. I'll be there when it all comes apart," he hissed, striding into the empty office floor of Christmas Imports.

Whispers in the Ledger

BRYAN AND PAM HAD ARRANGED to meet early the next day in his office, hoping to avoid attention before most people arrived.

Pam got there first to find the door ajar. She peeked through the crack, but there was no sign of Bryan. She hovered in the hallway, uncertain what to do next. The sound of footsteps behind her made her jump. *Bryan!* she thought, feeling the familiar flutter in her stomach whenever he appeared.

But when she turned, it was only Jim, the shipping clerk, walking briskly toward her. He slowed as he passed, giving her a polite nod and a puzzled look before continuing down the hall.

Pam's cheeks warmed. Loitering outside Bryan's office could raise questions if anyone else saw her — and she wasn't sure how she'd answer them. She considered heading back to her desk but hesitated. She wanted to be there the moment Bryan arrived.

I'll just go in, she decided. The door's open. *He won't mind.*

She slipped inside and quietly closed the door behind her. The small, dim room was freezing. *This place looks more like a storage cupboard than an office,* she thought, shivering.

She flicked on the desk lamp. It buzzed and flickered before casting a weak pool of light across the desk. She smiled faintly, remembering Bryan's joke about his office being haunted.

Pam stood awkwardly in the middle of the room, arms folded. *Where is he?* she wondered. She checked her watch — he was ten minutes late. Bryan was never late. He was always the one waiting for her to go on their café runs, and every morning he arrived at work at exactly the same time.

Bryan strode through the office floor, tall, confident, and handsome, exactly fifteen minutes after Pam arrived each day. She knew because she always watched for him.

He would stop to chat with the other employees as he crossed the floor. To the young men, he was like an older brother — talking football, cars, and weekend plans. To those with children, he was "Uncle Bryan," remembering birthdays and milestones. To his older colleagues, he was a considerate, loyal son.

Everyone was happy to see Bryan Higgin — but no one more so than Pam. Her desk was tucked away in the corner of the main floor, and every morning, before he turned down the hallway to his office, he would glance her way and wave with that dazzling smile.

Pam rubbed her hands together; the cold was giving her goosebumps. She checked the time again.

I'll look ridiculous just standing here when he arrives.

Her eyes drifted to the desk. *Maybe I'll sit down.*

No, that's too presumptuous. Oh, for goodness' sake, stop overthinking it, Pam.

She sighed, then sat.

A black ledger lay on the desk in front of her. This must be the book, she thought, running her hand over the worn cover.

Should I look at it? Pam debated again.

He asked me to look at it, she finally decided, and flipped the book open.

Bryan had highlighted numbers and columns with meticulous care. She wasn't an accountant, but even she could tell that things didn't add up—just as he'd said. As she flipped through more pages, she spotted several loose sheets tucked into the back.

She pulled one out. It was full of questions and thoughts—Bryan's, she assumed. She felt guilty reading them, but there were words underlined and capitalized that she couldn't ignore. Pam's eyes scanned the first page.

THE BOOKS. FREQUENT withdrawals, with **no** receipts. <u>Where is the money going??? What are they hiding?</u>

Jane whispered that John had snuck out—actually said "it's a secret." She looked SCARED. (Why? <u>Is she scared of John?</u>)

My "office" → no windows. Flickering bulb. Freezing. Meanwhile John sits in sunlight with his grand view. TWO WORLDS.

John Christmas = <u>flashy, indulgent.</u> Expensive lunches. Lavish purchases. Christmas shopping at Harrods. Most are barely able to make ends meet, while he shops at the most expensive department stores in London. Always the best for HIM. Public image: "frugal," "humble." → <u>LIES</u>. <u>HYPOCRISY.</u>

Smiles everywhere. Painted on. Too wide. Too long. <u>Forced cheer.</u>

"Family atmosphere." Ha. If John's the father, it's not love → it's FEAR.

At HOME too. Mary tells the children: "don't tell your dad, he'll be furious." Even they're AFRAID of him.

It all leads back to the money. Jane vague and flustered when questioned. WHY do they protect him?? WHY cover for him??

Rotten at the core.

THERE WERE SEVERAL more pages of notes, but Pam didn't need to read them all to understand why Bryan had looked so disturbed yesterday. She only ever saw John Christmas and Jane in passing; most of her time was spent on the main office floor. Bryan, on the other hand, was often summoned for meetings with them. He would have seen things

Pam never could. Seeing all of John Christmas's hypocrisy and lies must have eaten away at him for months.

"Poor Bryan," she whispered.

Pam slowly set the paper down. She had come here expecting to ease his mind — but now her own was racing. *Poor Jane. Poor Mary Christmas and her children.* Her kind, tender heart ached for all those John Christmas had hurt.

She jumped as the office door opened and Bryan stepped in, shutting it quietly behind him. Pam leapt from his chair.

"Please, don't get up," he said, shrugging off his mac. "Sorry I'm late. Missed the first bus." He gave her an apologetic smile.

"That's alright," said Pam. "Though... I'm afraid you might be cross with me. I peeked inside the ledger—and I found these notes." She gestured to the papers on the desk.

Bryan's eyes widened slightly, but he shook his head. "No, no. You were only doing what I asked. I'm just embarrassed by my disjointed scribblings—I wasn't expecting anyone else to see them. I hope it doesn't seem strange I wrote it down... I didn't know how else to make sense of it all."

"I understand," Pam said with a small smile. "But Bryan... this is awful. Worse than I ever imagined."

"I know." Bryan rubbed his temples. "I could hardly sleep last night."

"It's not right—the way Mr. Christmas treats people," Pam said, glancing at Bryan's notes.

"I agree. He has the reputation of a saint. Did you hear about that award he won? Outstanding Citizen of the Year, or something like that?" Pam nodded. "But it's all deceit. He's a hypocrite. We have the proof right here of what he's really like," Bryan said, patting the ledger. "My dad used to say, 'If something seems too good to be true, it probably is.'"

"We have to do something," she whispered.

"But what?" Bryan asked, his voice low and tired. "You start asking questions around here, and people shut down. And if word gets back to Mr. Christmas... well, you know how it goes. He'd find a way to get rid of us. People like us don't stand up to men like him."

Pam took a deep breath. "Then we go to the press. We expose him—before people here have the chance to cover for him. Before he sacks us. We'll probably lose our jobs either way. But at least we'd be telling the truth."

She shocked herself when she said the words out loud. There was a fire in her voice that she'd never heard before. The shy young secretary who once dreaded confrontation now sat with her shoulders squared and her eyes steady.

For a fleeting moment, she wondered where the sudden courage had come from. Maybe it was because someone like Bryan found her interesting—wanted to spend time with her, confided in her—that Pam suddenly felt strong. Confident. Capable. Like she mattered.

"The press? Wow, Pam, do you really think so?" Bryan's eyebrows rose in shock.

"Yes. We can't just stand by and let him keep doing these **monstrous** things," Pam answered firmly.

"You hit the nail on the head. What he does is **monstrous**," Bryan said, tucking the papers back inside the ledger.

He looked carefully at Pam. "Well, if we're going to do it—expose him—we need to do it right, and big." Bryan's resolve and confidence now matched Pam's.

"What do you have in mind?" she asked.

"We'll get in to see Graham Ellis, from *This Evening*. He's the best. I'll start making some phone calls."

Pam nodded. With her newfound confidence, she abruptly changed the subject.

"I'm having a little get-together at my flat on Christmas Eve, at seven. You're welcome to come. Just a buffet... sausage rolls, mince pies, that sort of thing," she added quickly.

"Oh, um... that's nice of you. I might be busy. You know—family stuff."

Pam tucked a loose strand of hair behind her ear. Bryan glanced over but said nothing. She always did that when she was unsure of what to say next—he'd noticed it before.

"Of course," she said, trying to keep the disappointment out of her voice.

There was a short pause, then Bryan offered a slight smile.

"Tell you what—why don't you write down your address, and I'll see if I can sneak away."

"Oh yes. I will," Pam said with a radiant smile.

Perfect Timing

PAM AND BRYAN SAT OPPOSITE Graham Ellis, the presenter of the country's most popular current affairs program, *This Evening*. Pam wasn't surprised that Bryan had managed to set up the meeting—nobody could refuse his charm and charisma.

Graham leaned back in his chair, scanning the pages in front of him. He had come across John Christmas and his importing company before. Earlier in the year, while working on a feature about local heroes—ordinary people who had performed acts of bravery or kindness—he had spotted John's name in a small village paper. The article described the award the mayor had given him. *Promising material,* Graham had thought at the time.

But when he reached out for an interview, John Christmas had brushed him off. The memory still grated. Few people dared to dismiss Graham Ellis. A man so eager to parade as a pillar of the community, yet unwilling to answer a few simple questions? It didn't sit right. Graham had built his reputation on shining a light into places others overlooked. Men who went out of their way to look like model citizens often had something to hide—he'd seen it before.

John Christmas wasn't a household name, but there were pieces here for a great story—from so-called local hero to lying, cheating businessman. Hypocrites irritated him more than almost anything. If there was rot beneath the polished surface, Graham Ellis would expose it.

The room was quiet, save for the steady ticking of the clock. Occasionally, Graham muttered under his breath: "This is great stuff."

When he finally finished, he stacked the pages with care and looked up at them. "I just need to ask a few questions."

Most were straightforward: "How long have you both worked at Christmas Imports?" and "Have you told anyone else about this?"

But then Graham looked straight at Pam. His tone shifted. "Does Mr. Christmas maintain appropriate relationships at work?"

Pam hesitated, brushing a strand of hair behind her ear. "Well... he treats everyone at work like family. He's very friendly."

Graham glanced down at his notepad, scribbling quickly. *Inappropriate work relationships. Overly friendly.*

"Here's what we're going to do," Graham said, sitting up straighter in his chair. "We'll break the story after Christmas. People want feel-good stories this time of year. Everyone's too full of goodwill right now for this to get them as worked up as we need them to be. We'll wait until January—when everyone's cold, broke, and looking for someone to blame. But we'll drop a little teaser first. On Christmas Eve. Give it a Scrooge spin."

Bryan nodded. "I think that makes sense. Timing is everything with a story like this. We want it to land properly." He glanced at Pam. "We owe it to everyone John Christmas has hurt to get this right. Oh, and one more thing, Mr. Ellis," Bryan added, turning back to Graham. "We'd rather remain anonymous sources. Do you think you can run the segment without naming us?"

Graham leaned back, considering. "That's better, actually. Viewers don't always trust nervous, first-time guests on live television. Anonymous employees pack a bigger punch — it makes the story feel broader, not personal." He tapped Bryan's notes on the desk. "This is more than enough for me to run with."

After Pam and Bryan stepped out of Graham's office, he buzzed his secretary. "Get me John Christmas at Christmas Imports, please."

A minute later, the company receptionist answered. "Mr. Christmas is not in the office presently. Would you like to leave a message?"

"Yes," Graham said crisply. "This is Graham Ellis from *This Evening*. I'm preparing an upcoming story involving Mr. Christmas. Please let him know he may contact my office if he wishes to make a statement."

When John returned later that afternoon, the receptionist handed him the note. He skimmed it, frowning. *Story involving me? Must be that local hero piece again.* He had already told Ellis he wasn't interested. With a sigh, he crumpled the paper into a ball and tossed it into the wastepaper basket.

"I HOPE WE'RE DOING the right thing," Pam said as she and Bryan stepped out into the chilly December air.

"Of course we are," Bryan replied gently.

They walked in silence for a few minutes, their breath misting in the cold.

"I... I have a Christmas present for you," Pam said, shyly pulling a neatly wrapped gift and card from her handbag.

Bryan's eyes widened.

"It's just a little thing," she added quickly, holding it out with nervous hands.

He hesitated, stiffening slightly as he took the gift and card.

Oh no. Am I being too forward? Heat crept up her neck. *Maybe this was a mistake. Maybe I've misunderstood everything.*

THAT EVENING, BRYAN sat alone as he slowly opened the card. *Happy Christmas. I hope you like the gift. Love from, Pam.*

He carefully peeled back the wrapping paper and lifted out a blue woolen scarf. He ran his hand slowly across the soft fabric. He read the card again, slower this time. It wasn't signed *yours truly, Pam* or *best wishes, Pam.* It said, *Love from, Pam.*

The Quiet Before Christmas

THE NEXT AFTERNOON, the main floor at Christmas Imports had fallen quiet. Just an hour earlier, the place had been alive with laughter, chatter, and Christmas music drifting from the radio in the corner.

No one had done much actual work—no one ever did on a day like this. John had arranged a generous buffet, and the break-room table had practically disappeared beneath plates of sausage rolls, mince pies, crumbly shortbread, and bowls of tangerines and nuts.

Now, the lights were dimmed, the music had stopped, and the only signs of the celebration were a few empty plates and a wrinkled red paper hat from a Christmas cracker. John had sent everyone home early to be with their families. The office wouldn't open again until January 2nd.

Only Jane and John remained.

"What are you still doing here?" John asked, poking his head around her office door.

"You made me jump," Jane said as she hurried to shove a red book bulging with papers into her desk drawer. With a firm push, the drawer slid closed and clicked into place. "I'm just finishing up a few things."

John's eyes lingered on the drawer she'd pulled her hand away from. "You look guilty. What are you up to?" he asked with a small laugh.

"Nothing," she replied, her gaze slipping away from his.

"Alright," John shrugged. "Well, you need to get going. What time does the last ferry leave?"

"I've got plenty of time. Are you trying to have the place to yourself?" she said with a chuckle.

Jane was spending Christmas week at her sister's house on the Isle of Wight. The trip involved a train to Portsmouth and a ferry ride across the Solent.

"Come on," John said, reaching for his coat. "I'm turning off the lights and walking you to the station."

Jane slipped her hands into her pockets as they stepped outside into the damp London air. They walked quietly for a while. Something about the silence between them unsettled John. It didn't seem right or normal. He glanced at Jane. She seemed distracted, uneasy.

"Everything alright?" he finally asked.

"Hmm? What did you say?"

"I asked if you're alright," John said.

"Yes, yes. I'm... yes, I'm alright. Just a little tired." She offered an unconvincing smile.

They walked quietly again.

"I think the party went well," John said, trying to break the awkward silence.

Jane felt relieved for the subject change. She latched on to the new conversation. *Act normal,* she told herself. *I can't tell him yet.*

"Everyone seemed happy," she agreed. "Did you notice some of the secretaries playing matchmaker? They made sure Pam and Bryan were sitting next to each other."

John grinned. "Can't say I did."

"If they end up together, it'll be because of the office Christmas party." Jane smiled, remembering how Pam's face had brightened when Bryan sat next to her.

"Wouldn't that be something." John took a deep breath, then slowly let it out. "I just love this time of year."

"I never would've guessed," Jane responded. "Hmmm... What gave it away—your name? The job? The life-sized reindeer in the foyer? You've built your whole life on Christmas," she said thoughtfully.

John laughed out loud, and at that very moment, the bells of Westminster Abbey pealed through the air, as if echoing his joy. The sound rolled across the city like a hymn—bold, hopeful, full of promise.

"I have a feeling about this Christmas," he said, his eyes scanning the rooftops beyond the Thames. "Like it's going to be extra special."

Jane rolled her eyes. "You say that every year."

"This feels different. Everything's ... lined up. The family's well. The team's in good spirits. Business is steady. I couldn't ask for more." He paused, then added more quietly, "I just feel at peace. Does that make sense?"

"Good for you," she said softly. "Peace doesn't come easily for most."

They turned the corner, and the Victory Arch that towered above the entrance of Waterloo station came into view, its stone-carved soldiers standing guard beneath Britannia's watchful gaze.

There was a steady stream of travelers hurrying in and out of the arch. Some were the usual commuters, eager to get home to their loved ones. Others were families with arms full of parcels and suitcases, the children bundled in coats and mittens. The scent of diesel and pine mingled in the air. Somewhere in the distance, a brass band played a few wobbly bars of *O Come All Ye Faithful*.

John clapped his hands together. "Well, you're off on your adventure. Tell your nieces Father Christmas sends his regards."

"Oh, I will," Jane said with a grin. "No peeking under the tree until the 25th," she added.

"That's no fun," he replied.

"Someone has to make sure you behave yourself, John Christmas," Jane called out as she disappeared through the archway.

John watched her slip into the stream of travelers. Then, for a moment, he kept his eyes fixed on where she'd stood, as if hoping she might turn back. Something wasn't right. What wasn't she telling him? *Maybe she's just tired*, he thought, recalling what she'd said earlier. *Perhaps she'll feel better after some rest over Christmas*, he told himself as she disappeared from view.

The light drizzle caught the lampposts, which were beginning to flicker to life, glinting like strands of tinsel in the mist. It was as if the city itself was preparing for Christmas. Remembering that tomorrow was Christmas Eve made John feel cheerful again.

This Christmas is going to be one for the books, John thought contently as he began his own trip home.

Scrooge Among Us

THE BIG DAY WAS FAST approaching, and Christmas Eve celebrations were in full swing at the Christmas home! Mary and John were the proud parents of five children, two of whom were now married with children of their own. John loved being a dad—but being a grandad was nothing short of magical to him. With the arrival of John's parents, Matthew and Sarah Christmas, the home was bursting at the seams, but John wouldn't have it any other way.

After a feast fit for a king, John pulled his dad aside. "*This Evening's* just starting. Let's sneak away and catch a bit. Wait till you see Graham Ellis on the new TV—it's like he's sitting right in your living room," he said with a proud grin.

"I could do with a sit-down," Matthew chuckled, tugging at his belt. "I think I overdid it a bit."

Hector followed them into the living room. He sprawled on the floor in front of the television, digging through a tin of chocolates in search of his favorite.

"Go easy there, Hector boy," said Matthew Christmas. "You'll make yourself sick after that big meal."

"I'm not even full yet," Hector said, pulling a chocolate in a shiny purple wrapper from the tin.

"It's starting!" John exclaimed.

"Good evening," said Graham Ellis from the screen. "Just one day to go now until the big day, and whether you're still elbow-deep in wrapping paper or waiting for the in-laws to descend, why not take a break and join us for our Christmas Eve special?"

John shook his head in awe. "See what I mean? Like he's talking right to us."

They watched as Graham followed Mr. Tompkins, a Royal Mail worker who had been sorting letters and cards at London's Mount Pleasant Mail Centre for 38 years. "He might just be the busiest man in England this week," Graham joked.

After a segment on that year's most popular toys—complete with Tiny Tears dolls and wind-up robots—and a cheerful rendition of *Rudolph the Red-Nosed Reindeer* by a local community choir in bobble hats and red scarves, Graham Ellis returned to the camera. His tone had noticeably changed.

"Looking ahead to next week—and keeping with the Christmas theme—we have a story about a company called Christmas Imports, run by the family it's named after," said Graham.

"I wonder what this is about," John said, raising his eyebrows. "Hush, everyone—Graham's saying something about Christmas Imports," he called out.

The noisy house fell quiet. All eyes turned to the television.

"The company is well known for its family values," Graham continued. "It has provided honest and quality service for generations."

Mary smiled proudly and gave John's shoulder a gentle pat.

"But now, several employees have come forward with concerns about the owner's character—allegations of financial misconduct, an extravagant lifestyle... and inappropriate relationships in the workplace," Graham said solemnly.

Mary's hand flew to her face; she gasped.

A photo of John filled the screen.

"Grandad!" squeaked little Timothy.

John's brow furrowed. "What on earth..." And then, with a sick jolt, he remembered the crumpled note from Graham Ellis in his wastebasket. *That's what it was about...*

"Well, that's shocking. With a name like Christmas, you'd expect a little more goodwill," said Graham's co-host, as the camera cut to his wide-eyed expression. If John didn't know better, he'd swear the man was staring straight at him.

"Yes, you won't want to miss this," Graham added. "One source even claims that Mrs. Christmas has warned her children to 'beware of their father's temper.'" He shook his head slightly, careful not to reveal too much too soon. *Just enough to make them tune in,* he reminded himself.

"On this Christmas Eve, while most of us are gathering with loved ones, it seems one family man may be living a double life. Do we have a Scrooge among us?" Graham said, his mouth tightening into a grim line.

The words lingered in the air, heavy as coal in a stocking.

"Turn it off," Harvey said sharply, glancing at Hazel, who was closest to the TV.

The room fell eerily silent. Even the youngest children could sense something was wrong.

A log cracked in the fireplace, and then everyone started talking at once.

"Who's been snooping around in the books?" asked Matthew, his voice gruff and low.

"What do they mean about Daddy's temper?" Holly asked, tears welling in her eyes.

"Utter nonsense," said Sarah Christmas, banging her fist on the oak console of the television set.

"But that's not even true, is it? Why would they say that on telly if it's not true?" asked Hector, setting the tin of chocolates down on the coffee table.

"John..." Mary whispered, her voice barely audible. "What are they talking about?"

John sat silently in his armchair, staring at the blank television screen. Questions raced through his mind, refusing to rest. But the one that returned again and again was the same: who had done this to him? Who were these "several employees" that had come forward—and why? Did they truly see him as a fraud? Or was this nothing more than a spiteful attack, meant to tear him down?

The smoky, shadowy form of Krampus crouched on the oak TV console, watching the Christmas family unravel. He clapped his twisted claws together in delight. Childish, perhaps—but since none of those fools could see him, why hold back?

A year had passed since he last stepped inside this house, though he'd never been far from its affairs. He had other ways of knowing. And now, at last, everything was falling into place. Graham Ellis had done his part brilliantly, and the family's reaction was better still.

"Not even your jolly, fat friend can save you from this, Johnny-boy," he sneered, a crooked smile curling through the smoke.

What next? He could linger here and watch the evening fall further into chaos. Tempting. Or he could spread a little more mischief elsewhere. He had waited so long for this moment—why not savor it?

Then Mary Christmas lifted her head. Her eyes swept the room—and for a moment, impossibly, they seemed to fix on him. She shivered, rubbing her arms as she continued to stare at the oak console. Krampus froze. She couldn't see him. None of them could. And yet... she always had a way of sensing him when he was near. It unsettled him. That woman annoyed him almost as much as her goody-two-shoes husband.

Her gaze held just long enough to make him uneasy. That was all it took to tip the scales. He couldn't risk her spoiling his plans.

"Everything's going fabulously here," he muttered, baring his crooked teeth. With that, his smoky form slipped through the crack of the front door, leaving behind a faint trace of sulfur—and an abundance of bad will.

Peace on Earth?

IT CAN'T BE TRUE, CAN it? Hector glanced at the television set but quickly looked away before anyone noticed. He scanned the room instead. The house was warm, cozy—filled with nice things. *Is that what extravagant means?*

Guilt crept in. Last Christmas, when everything had gone wrong and everyone thought he'd ruined the day on purpose, Dad gave him a chance to explain.

But now... Dad just sat there, saying nothing. Not defending himself. Not even looking angry. *Does that mean he's guilty?* Hector swallowed the lump rising in his throat.

The telephone rang; it seemed louder and more shrill than usual. Mary glanced at John, her stomach tightening, before getting up to answer it.

"Hello," she said, fighting to keep her voice steady. There was a pause. "Michael," she finally said. "You know it's all made up..." Her voice quivered slightly. "Why don't you just wait until this is all cleared up?"

Another pause.

"All right. Well, if you change your mind... Yes, I understand. Wish Carol and the girls a Happy Christmas. Goodbye."

John spoke his first words since the teaser had aired. "Was that Michael from the office?"

Mary nodded.

"What did he want?"

"Let's talk about it later," she replied, glancing around the room at the family.

"Mary, if Michael needs something or there's a problem at work, you need to let me know."

She hesitated. "He said he'll be handing in his notice as soon as the office opens."

John had no time to react because just then, the telephone rang again, making Mary flinch.

"I'll get it," John said, rising slowly from his chair.

Mary watched him cross the room. Only minutes earlier, those awful things had been said about him, and already the words seemed to weigh him down. His shoulders sagged. His steps were slow and tired.

"Hello," they heard him say. A pause. "George... I see. I'm sorry you feel that way. I understand... Goodbye."

He replaced the receiver with a heavy hand.

"Who was it?" Mary asked, now standing beside him.

"George Carter — you remember him? We've had him over for dinner a few times."

"Yes," Mary answered with a nod.

"He said he doesn't see how we can keep working together — that it'd be bad for his business. If he's shaken, then other clients will take it even worse." John's voice was flat.

"We've done business with him for years," Matthew added, frowning. "He was one of my best clients."

"It didn't take long for the disloyalty to begin," Sarah said, fire in her voice.

"I'm sure that's just the start of it. The whole country would've been watching a Graham Ellis Christmas special," Matthew said grimly.

Sarah glanced at John, who sat with his head in his hands, and shot Matthew a warning look. "That's not helping," she snapped.

Mary laid her hand on the phone. "We're going to take it off the hook for now." She sat back down in her armchair with a heavy sigh. "Who do you think did this? Who went to Graham Ellis? Obviously, there's some truth to it. Someone knows about the spending that..." she hesitated, "you keep quiet."

John looked up. "I'm not sure. I have my ideas, though."

"Who?" Mary pressed.

"The new accountant we hired at the beginning of the year, Bryan. He had complete access to the books." John shook his head. "He doesn't seem the type, though. If there were a popularity contest at work, he'd win it. He just seems too nice. But sometimes those are the ones you least suspect."

"Wait a minute—did you say Bryan?" asked Mary.

"Yes," John answered. "Bryan Higgin."

Mary's eyes widened. "I met him when I was in Jane's office a couple of weeks ago. John, I really felt like something was off with him. I should have said something."

"Why give a new accountant free rein in the books?" Matthew asked in a low voice.

"It's not usually a problem," John answered. "When the accountants ask about the unaccounted-for money, Jane tells them to put it under charitable giving, and that's the end of it."

"This is all fishy," Matthew almost growled. "There has to be more than this Bryan fellow involved. Ellis said, 'several employees.'"

"You know journalists," John said. "They could be exaggerating, sensationalizing things. I need to contact Terrance, my solicitor — see if he can do some digging around. Maybe he can find out more about Bryan."

"And ask him where we stand legally — if there's any way to stop them from airing this nonsense," Matthew said, his jaw tightening. "An importing business is built on reputation," he added, shaking his head. "Without our good name, we're finished."

Heather watched the younger members of the family while the adults talked. It was Christmas Eve, yet instead of excitement for the day ahead, the children looked afraid and confused. They sat quietly, listening to words like *solicitor* and *unaccounted for money*—words that didn't belong in a room filled with tinsel and Christmas lights. Where was the magic of Christmas that was usually so abundant in this home on Christmas Eve?

Timothy had climbed into Harvey's lap and buried his face against his father's shoulder. Hector sat stiffly on the floor, staring at the carpet. Holly sat close to Hazel, twisting the ribbon at the waist of her dress with nervous fingers. Even Heather's own usually lively toddler sat quietly beside her, turning the pages of a picture book.

Heather finally spoke. "You won't be able to reach anyone tonight, Dad—not until after Boxing Day. We'll sort this all out then. But tonight is Christmas Eve, and the little ones need to feel it."

She forced a smile. "Come on, let's make some hot cocoa and get everyone settled down to read the nativity story."

"Yes, yes, you're right, Heather love," John said with a small smile.

Everyone went about their business trying to act normal, but the mood in the house was tense and fragile.

Mary busied herself in the kitchen, but her eyes kept drifting toward the living room where John sat, silent and still. She couldn't shake the image of him on the television screen. *How much had that thing cost, anyway? And what did they mean by inappropriate relationships in the workplace?*

Her mind spun with questions, each one louder than the last, until she struggled to focus on anything. As she lifted a mug from the cupboard, it slipped from her hand and shattered on the floor.

"Oh no!" she cried, already reaching for the broom.

"Mum, sit down. Let me take care of it," Heather said gently, taking the broom from her.

Mary didn't argue. She was too tired. She sank into the armchair opposite John and closed her eyes.

"What did they mean, 'Mrs. Christmas has warned her children to beware of their father's temper?'" John asked quietly.

Mary opened her eyes. "I honestly don't know, John."

"Someone must have heard you say something like that, Mary."

She racked her brain, trying to recall anything she might have said—anything that could've been twisted into that accusation. Then her eyes widened. *It couldn't be that... could it?*

She finally spoke. "A few weeks ago, when I came into town and we went shopping and to that nice restaurant—remember?"

John nodded. *'Extravagant lifestyle,'* Graham Ellis's voice echoed in his head.

"I was talking to Jane, and I mentioned that Holly couldn't see any difference between the old TV and the new one. And I said—" she hesitated, "— 'don't tell your dad, he'll be furious.'"

"You said that to Jane?" John asked, trying to make sense of everything.

A movement at the doorway made them both turn. Holly stood there, her eyes wide with shock.

"I'm so sorry, Dad. It's all my fault," she said.

"No, no. Holly, dear," Mary said quickly, getting up. "Of course it's not your fault."

"Do you think I have a temper, Mary? Do you really have to warn the children not to tell me things?" John asked, his voice trembling slightly.

"No, John. It was just a joke. A bad one."

Heather entered the room carrying a tray of mugs filled with cocoa. She set them carefully on the table and smiled, trying to lighten the mood again.

"Here we go, then. All ready. Dad, shall I get the Bible off the shelf so you can read the Christmas story?"

John looked at her and gave a strained smile. "Why don't you give it to Grandad this year, Heather love?" Holly's eyes darted to her dad. Her whole life he had been the one to read the nativity story on Christmas Eve. She even remembered one Christmas when he'd had a bad cold, he still insisted on reading it to the family. She didn't understand all the grown-up talk from earlier, but she knew enough to understand that something was terribly wrong.

Silent Night

SOME MILES AWAY IN London, another Christmas Eve was unfolding. While the Christmas family huddled together in unease in Windlesham, Bryan Higgin strode toward Pam's flat with a grin on his face.

The world around him was quiet, save for the occasional black taxi or red double-decker bus splashing through puddles in the road. It wasn't often the city felt this peaceful at this hour. But after the December rush of shopping, festivities, and parties, it seemed as though everything had finally paused to catch its breath before Christmas Day.

Bryan was in high spirits. Graham Ellis had done a fantastic job with the teaser. John Christmas would soon get what he deserves.

He strutted along the pavement, which glistened in the lamplight after the rain. For a while he saw no one, until an older man appeared, shuffling toward him with a Yorkshire terrier on a lead. The little dog barked and yapped furiously as they passed. Bryan grinned and waved as though he were the star of his own parade. The dog walker stared at him, stunned, then quickly lowered his head and hurried on. Bryan laughed out loud, the sound carrying down the empty street. *Ah, what a perfect night,* he thought contently.

His smile faded as he reached the address Pam had written down. Suddenly, he didn't feel quite so full of himself. Being around Pam always complicated things. He looked up at the block of flats towering above him. Most of the windows glowed warmly, some framed by open curtains and brightly lit Christmas trees. Somewhere on the third floor was Pam.

He paused at number 301 and pulled the blue scarf from his coat pocket. *It'll look strange if I don't wear it*, he reasoned. As he looped it around his neck, a faint, sweet scent drifted up. *Strawberry. Shampoo, perhaps. It smells like her.*

He shook his head sharply. *Don't think of her like that. Don't think of her at all. They always end up hurting you.*

"Bryan, you made it," Pam beamed as she opened the door. She noticed immediately that he was wearing the scarf she had given him. The soft blue fabric made his pale blue eyes look even more striking.

"Hello, Pam," he said with a smile.

Pam drew a quick, steadying breath. *Oh, that smile.* For a moment she forgot the bustle behind her.

She led him inside and introduced him to her other guests. They both stood awkwardly in the kitchen for a moment as Pam's friends drifted back into their own conversations.

"Oh, thank you for the gift," Bryan said, breaking the silence.

"Of course, I hope you like it."

"Very much—blue's my favorite color. I bought you a little something too." He handed her an oblong white box.

Pam blushed as she took it.

"Go on, open it," Bryan encouraged.

A sweet scent of pastry wafted up even before she lifted the lid. Inside were two neat rows of golden custard tarts.

"Thought you might miss our café runs over the holidays," Bryan said with a proud grin.

Pam looked up, tucking her hair behind her ear, her cheeks burning. "Thank you," she said softly. Her throat felt tight, as though she might laugh, cry, or fling her arms around him all at once. Instead, she set the box carefully on the counter, her fingers trembling. *Bryan. In her flat. With a thoughtful gift just for her.* She could hardly believe it.

She cleared her throat, reaching for something—anything—to say. "Did you... did you see the teaser tonight?"

"Yes," Bryan said with an easy nod. "I thought Graham handled it well."

Pam hesitated. She leaned closer and lowered her voice. "I think I'll need to start looking for a new job after Christmas."

Bryan briefly glanced around her flat. It was small, the furnishings worn—probably hand-me-downs, he guessed—but everything was neat and comfortable. On the wall hung several framed photos of Pam with her parents. He knew from their chats at the café and the park that she was an only child.

Seeing her here, in this modest home, smiling out from those photographs, caused his earlier exuberance to dim. Had he ruined her chance to make a decent living? She'd certainly lose her job at Christmas Imports, and finding another could be difficult. *Nobody likes a whistleblower. No going back now*, he firmly reminded himself.

"You and me both," Bryan whispered back. "Hey, maybe we can both find a new job near the café and still do our morning break together," he joked.

"Yes, yes," Pam agreed hopefully. The thought of still going to the café with Bryan was the happiest thing she could imagine.

"Do you still think we did the right thing?" she whispered again.

Bryan didn't answer right away. He met her eyes and held them for a moment. "Yes," he said at last, his voice steady. "It was the right thing to do. It wasn't easy, but John Christmas left us with no choice."

Something in the way he said it — the quiet certainty in his voice, the steadiness of his gaze — steadied her too. Pam straightened her shoulders. The doubt that had been creeping in began to fade. Bryan believed they'd done the right thing. That meant she could believe it too.

"Hey, Pam," a voice called out from the other room. "We've all voted for getting a game of Monopoly going."

"Okay," Pam chuckled. She turned to Bryan. "What do you say to a game of Monopoly?"

"Sounds good! Nothing like good old Monopoly to spark a few arguments on Christmas Eve," he said with a laugh.

Saint or Monster?

THE STOCKINGS HAD BEEN hung and the treats left for Father Christmas and the reindeer. Everyone was tucked in their beds, but John sat alone in the living room, the dying fire the only light. He told himself not to wallow—but the weight of disappointment was too heavy to ignore. Just yesterday, he'd stood in the train station thinking this Christmas would be "one for the books."

"One for the books, all right," he scoffed.

His eyes drifted to the television set. In the half-light, it seemed even bigger. Was it so wrong to treat yourself now and then? He'd told everyone the new TV was for the whole family. But deep down, he knew it had been mostly for him. Still—he worked hard. Didn't he deserve something once in a while?

The cruelest irony was that just last week, he'd made a quiet donation to the children's hospital—a large one. No name. No recognition. He hadn't done it for praise. But public humiliation? That was his reward?

Accusations like the ones he'd heard tonight could destroy a man. Losing the business, he could almost accept. It felt as though it was already slipping through his fingers with the phone calls they'd received—and who knew how many others had tried to get through?

But what cut him to the core was the questions that wouldn't leave him: would his family ever look at him the same way again?

Did they believe it? Was it all nonsense? Or had he crossed lines without even noticing—too casual at work, too sharp at home? Could Mary still trust him? Could his children? His grandchildren?

And what about his father? The man who had entrusted him with the family business? Generations had run Christmas Imports, and none of them had made a mess of it like him.

John dropped his head into his hands and rubbed his temples, but the thoughts raged like a storm with no end in sight.

After a while, he looked up at the picture above the fireplace — the painting of his ancestor, Thomas William Christmas. In the flickering light, he could barely make out

Thomas's smile behind the gold frame. But he didn't need to see it; the image of Thomas was etched into his memory.

Every Christmas Day, John would gather his children—and now his grandchildren—and tell them the story behind their unusual surname. How their family had cherished the season for generations. How, long ago, the Christmas family hosted grand celebrations and, according to legend, even saved Christmas a time or two. The story they all loved most was Thomas's.

The Christmas family didn't just believe in the magic of Christmas—they believed in guardian angels. And some, it was said, had the rare gift of seeing theirs. John believed, with all his heart, that Thomas William Christmas was his guardian angel.

The first time John saw Thomas, he was only four years old. His mother had taken him and his siblings for a spring walk in the nearby woods. They had been wandering and playing for a while when a storm appeared out of nowhere. The wind howled, sending leaves and blossoms swirling through the air, and the rain poured down.

John's mother quickly scooped him up in her arms and grabbed the hands of her other children. The rain blurred her vision, making it hard to tell which way led home. Panic rose in her throat.

But through the storm, John saw someone. "Who's that man, Mummy?" he asked, repeating the question until his mother finally responded.

"Be quiet now, John. Let Mummy concentrate," she said, her voice tight with fear.

"He says to go that way," said young John, keeping his eyes fixed on the man who seemed to be guiding them. With no other choice, his mother followed the directions John repeated from the stranger. Moments later, they were safely home. John wouldn't know until he was older that the man he'd seen was Thomas.

There had been other moments since—subtle, quiet encounters during life's hardest trials. Like the time he was in the hospital waiting room, when Mary went into early labor with Holly. John had been terrified of losing them both. And then, without fanfare, Thomas appeared—sitting silently beside him. A quiet reassurance he wasn't alone. Most of the time John couldn't see Thomas, but he could feel his calming presence; now and then, Thomas came to him in dreams. But tonight—nothing.

The fire sputtered. Shadows swallowed the frame above the hearth.

Thomas was gone.

Had he disappointed him? Had he fallen so far that even his guardian angel had turned away?

The last ember crumbled to ash, the smoke curling upward, leaving the room as cold and dark as the thoughts in John's mind.

The Answer Before the Prayer

HORACE KNOCKED SOFTLY on the living room door at the North Pole.

"Come in," Martha called.

Nicholas and Martha sat close together on the green velvet couch, sipping hot cocoa.

"Horace, what brings you here?" Nicholas asked warmly.

"I'm sorry to bother you. You haven't been back long from the deliveries and I'm sure you're tired," Horace said gently. "But I'm afraid I have some... unpleasant news."

"Oh?" Nicholas set his mug down.

Martha's eyes widened. "What is it, Horace?"

"There are reports of an upcoming segment on a popular news program," Horace began. "It's about Mr. Christmas — it contains some deeply troubling accusations."

Nicholas sat up straight.

"Dishonesty in business," Horace continued. "Inappropriate relationships, questions about his character..." His voice trailed off as he stared at the floor.

"Oh no," Martha gasped.

"I knew Cavan would pull out all the stops, but this... this is worse than I imagined," Nicholas said, rubbing his tired eyes.

"You don't know it was Cavan," Martha said quickly. She could never quite believe all the things people said about him. To her, he was still funny, kind Cavan — flawed, yes, but not beyond hope.

Horace cleared his throat. "Well... I'm afraid there's something we missed. It didn't seem important at the time, but at the start of the year Christmas Imports hired a new accountant. After a closer look... we believe the accountant is Cavan. He must have taken on his old form to infiltrate the company—and frame Mr. Christmas. He's going by the name Bryan Higgin. He's even dragged a young secretary into it."

"Oh, Cavan..." Martha whispered. "Why would he get a poor young secretary mixed up in his scheming?" she asked, turning to Nick.

"Because he's clever — very clever," Nicholas said gravely. "Think about it — his accusations will look more credible with someone else backing him up. And who better than a nice young secretary? It makes John look even worse."

Martha nodded as tears welled in her eyes.

"Still, it was a bit sloppy of him to go in looking like his old self," Nicholas continued.

"Well, he did disguise himself a little—changed his hair color, put on some glasses, and so on. But his eyes always give him away. I blame myself entirely. We should have been paying closer attention," Horace said, his tone heavy with regret.

It was true. No matter who Cavan became—Krampus, Bryan, or any other creature he imagined—his eyes never changed. His pale, icy blue eyes were distinctive. Unforgettable.

"No, don't feel bad. None of us were expecting this," Nicholas said with a kind smile.

Horace nodded, then went on. "This has hit the Christmas family hard. And it's gone all the way to the top." He pointed upward. "The angels are on it—but they're having trouble reaching John. He's in a very low, dark place."

Nicholas nodded slowly, absorbing the news. "Alright, alright," he murmured. Then, with a hint of hope, he added, "But no need to panic. John's not the only one in that family with the gift."

THAT CHRISTMAS EVE, when Holly went to bed, her heart felt heavy. The usual excitement she felt for Christmas Day had been replaced by fear and confusion. She had never seen her dad so unhappy. Was it her fault — for saying the picture on the new television didn't look any different? The thought made her chest ache.

She knelt beside her bed and prayed the most earnest prayer she'd ever prayed. Her whispered words seemed to vanish into the quiet house. For a moment she wondered if God had even heard her at all.

Usually on Christmas Eve, her head would be full of happy thoughts — Father Christmas soaring through the night sky, reindeer hooves tapping across rooftops. But this year, all she could picture was her dad sitting silently in his armchair.

She cried herself to sleep.

When sleep finally came, her dreams carried her to the Christmas family living room. The soft glow of the tree lights was the only thing illuminating the space. She was curled up in the armchair where her mum usually sat, and across from her sat Thomas William Christmas.

Holly knew she was dreaming, but she was so happy to see him. Thomas always knew what to do.

"Thomas, I'm so glad you're here," she whispered. "I didn't know who else to talk to. I tried praying... I think I did it wrong."

Thomas leaned back in his chair and crossed his arms. His presence alone calmed her.

"No such thing as a wrong prayer, Holly," he said. "Why would you think you did it wrong?"

She looked up at him, tears on her cheeks. "Because I don't think it worked. I think my dad is still sad and in trouble."

Thomas gave a small, knowing smile. "Let me tell you something special about prayers that most people don't know. Sometimes they're answered before they're even spoken. A lifetime of prayers is part of one moment to God."

Holly tilted her head. "How can something be answered before it's asked?"

"It's hard to explain in a way that fits into time," he said. "But think of it like a story. God already knows the whole book—even the parts we haven't read yet. And when He hears a prayer, sometimes He says, 'I've already woven the answer into chapter eight.'"

She sat quietly, thinking it over. "So... does that mean God knew I'd pray about Dad?"

Thomas nodded. "He knew your heart would break for him. And He's already been working on answers — long before you were even born."

Holly looked down at her hands. A fresh wave of sadness washed over her as she remembered how lost her dad had seemed that evening.

"Why didn't you just stop all the bad things before they happened?"

Thomas's smile softened. "We can never take away free will — or God's will. Number one rule of guardian angels."

Holly nodded slowly as tears continued to trickle down her cheeks.

"Your dad's forgotten who he is. You need to help him remember," Thomas said.

"But... how can I do that?" Holly asked, wiping away the tears.

Thomas gave a small, confident smile. "I think you'll find a way." His voice was growing fainter.

"Cheer up, Holly, it's Christmas tomorrow — and your birthday," he said, so softly now she could barely hear him.

Thomas's words settled over her like a warm blanket. The lights on the tree shimmered, soft and golden. When she looked again, Thomas was no longer in the chair opposite her. But somehow, Holly felt he was still close by.

What Holly Wished For

JOHN HAD BEEN AWAKE most of the night, and exhaustion only added to his growing sense of despair. But despite everything, he tried to put on a brave face—for his family, and especially for Holly. Today was her tenth birthday, and he was determined not to ruin it.

He smiled and made small talk about the presents and the Christmas dinner, but he wasn't fooling anyone—especially not Mary.

Mary watched him closely. Usually, John was the first to wake on Christmas Day, humming carols while helping her peel the potatoes, and laughing the loudest at the Christmas cracker jokes. This year, when the jokes were read, he offered only a polite chuckle.

He was trying—Mary knew that—but the light in his eyes had dimmed. And she didn't know how to bring it back.

The past two Christmases had been difficult ones for the Christmas family, which was ironic, because Christmas meant the world to them; they loved celebrating it. Not in a showy, flashy kind of way—no, that wasn't what it was about. Their joy came from something deeper: a love for what Christmas truly meant.

So why had the last few Christmases been so challenging? *Are we being tested?* Mary wondered.

At two o'clock, as they did every year, the Christmas celebrations paused for Holly's birthday.

"Make a wish," Mary said hopefully after the family had sung "Happy Birthday" to Holly.

Holly stared at the ten pink candles for a moment and then blew them out.

"What did you wish for?" Hazel whispered to Holly.

Holly leaned in closer to Hazel. "I wished that Dad could be happy again," she whispered. Holly hadn't forgotten Thomas's words in her dream. She knew wishing alone wasn't enough—and she already had an idea.

Just then, the family heard the clear chime of Father Christmas's sleigh bells on the roof—fulfilling his promise to John to deliver Holly's birthday presents on her special day.

"I don't know of any other child in the world who gets such a delivery," Mary said with a smile and tears of gratitude brimming in her eyes.

Father Christmas always carried with him the magic of the season—an unmistakable spark of joy and hope. As the sound of the sleigh bells faded into the cool afternoon air, even John's spirits seemed to lift a little.

"Come on, Holly love. Let's see what Father Christmas left for you," he said.

While Holly's birthday wish was for her father's happiness, across the water someone else was thinking of John too. But her thoughts were not of wishes—they were of secrets, and she knew the time had come to bring the truth to light.

ON THE ISLE OF WIGHT, Jane returned from the phone box for the third time that day.

"You still can't get through?" asked her sister.

Jane shook her head and began to unbutton her coat. "No. I don't know if the line's down or if there's a problem with their phone... Either way, I need to get back to London."

"You won't be able to get the ferry until after Boxing Day. You might as well try to relax. You can try the phone again tomorrow," her sister said gently.

Jane pressed her lips together. "I just wish I could speak to John. I warned him this would come out eventually. I won't stay quiet any longer."

Her sister folded her arms. "You've kept his secrets long enough. Maybe it's time people knew the truth—whether he likes it or not."

The Secrets in the Red Book

MARY HAD INSISTED THEY leave the telephone off the hook until after Boxing Day.

"We're not letting all that nonsense ruin Christmas," she said firmly.

Nonsense. The word lingered in John's mind. Did Mary truly believe that, or was she only being kind—too forgiving, as always?"

The day after Boxing Day, John stood in the hallway, the phone receiver heavy in his hand. For a long moment, he simply stared at it. Once he put the receiver back on the hook, he was certain it would start ringing—and even more certain that most of the calls would not be pleasant. But first, there was a call he needed to make.

"Can we stop the segment from airing?" he asked Terrance, his solicitor. Plenty of damage had already been done with the teaser, but if they could stop the full broadcast, John might still have some reputation to salvage.

"Yes, yes — I think we can stop it," Terrance said. His optimism made John feel calmer than he had in days. "Just produce some documents — invoices, receipts — that will clear up the financial allegations. Then the other..." he paused, "...attacks on your character will seem less believable."

"I don't have anything like that," John said flatly.

The line went quiet. John imagined Terrance pinching the bridge of his nose, fighting to keep his voice level.

"What do you mean you don't have anything like that?" Terrance asked, more sharply than he intended.

"I cover the expenses, pay wages, and donate what's left. I deliberately don't keep records — so the giving stays anonymous."

When Terrance spoke again, his concern was harder to hide.

"Without proof, it's just our word against theirs. I won't sugarcoat it, John. This doesn't look good. Did anyone from *This Evening* reach out for a statement? If not, we might be able to argue unfair treatment."

"Yes, they did reach out," John admitted quietly. "I thought it was about another piece Ellis was doing earlier in the year. So, I ignored it."

There was a pause on the line. Then Terrance's voice, low and steady: "So they asked for a response, and you gave none?"

"Yes."

Terrance sighed. "John, that changes everything. They'll say you were contacted and chose not to comment. To the public, that's as good as admitting guilt."

The brief calm John had managed to gather shattered. The panic — the heaviness of Christmas Eve — crashed back over him.

"So, what now?" he asked.

"Clients and employees are already backing away. I don't know how we can restore confidence. I'm not sure the company can survive this," Terrance said slowly, letting the words sink in. "I'm so sorry, John."

John paced the hallway, as far as the telephone cord would allow.

The line was quiet until Terrance spoke again. "You may need to shut the company down — while there's still something left to salvage," he said gently.

The words hit hard, but John didn't put up a fight. Terrance knew what he was doing. John knew that.

"I think you need to issue a statement," Terrance continued. "Maybe even hold a small press conference. Do you want me to arrange that?"

"Yes. Thank you, Terrance. I've made such a mess of this," John said quietly. "I never saw any of it coming. You must think I'm a fool."

"No, of course not," Terrance replied. "Anyone could have made the same mistakes."

John cleared his throat, trying to steady himself. "I wonder if you could do something else for me."

"What do you need?"

"Could you have your people do some digging around? See who's behind all of this. Especially look into a new accountant we hired at the beginning of the year — Bryan Higgin."

"Yes, of course," Terrance said. "I'll be in touch soon."

The phone kept ringing: friends and family checking on Mary and the children, employees expressing disappointment and saying they'd be handing in their notice when the office reopened. Other news outlets called, asking if John wanted to "tell his side of the story." Those calls—along with Terrance's follow-ups about the statement and press conference—left John looking pale and drawn.

"Let's take it off the hook again," Mary said, gently squeezing his hand.

"No. No, Mary, love—we can't, in case Terrance rings again."

"Well, let's at least get you out for a little break. A walk or a drive. Hazel can answer the phone and take a message from Terrance if he calls."

"I don't know, Mary. Some of those calls..." He hesitated. "Some of those people aren't exactly kind, and they ask a lot of questions."

"We'll tell Hazel not to answer questions or ask questions. Just be polite and take a message. If people get mean, she can hang up. She can handle it," Mary reassured.

John reluctantly agreed to go out for just half an hour. Hazel would man the phone.

THE FERRY DOCKED AT Portsmouth Harbor. Jane was on the move before the ropes were tied. Straight to the station, and then to Christmas Imports. No detours. Her suitcase would wait. What mattered was getting her information about John into Graham Ellis's hands—before the segment aired.

The first thing she did when she arrived at Christmas Imports was pick up the phone and dial the Christmas home.

Hazel answered after two rings. "Hello."

"Hello, may I speak to John, please?"

"He's not here right now. Would you like to leave a message?"

"Yes, please—make sure he gets this as soon as possible," Jane said, her voice rushed and a little breathless. "Tell him Jane from the office called."

Hazel picked up a notepad and jotted: **Jane**.

"Let him know I've got more information, and I'm taking it to Graham Ellis."

Hazel froze; her pencil tip pressed against the paper. Should she write it exactly like that? She chewed her lip, then forced herself to keep going: **More info to Ellis.**

"And... just tell him I'm sorry. About everything."

Hazel's hand hovered over the page. Sorry for what? Sorry about Graham Ellis? Sorry to her dad? Mary's instructions echoed in her mind: *Be polite, don't answer questions, don't ask questions. Just take a message. Hang up if they get nasty.*

For a long moment Hazel stared at the paper, wishing she could ask Jane to explain. At last, she added a single word, her writing smaller and shakier than the rest: **Sorry.**

Jane set the receiver down and leaned back in her chair. She closed her eyes, pressing her hands against her temples with a weary sigh. But then, with renewed resolve, she lifted the telephone once more. The rotary clicked slowly, each turn loud in the quiet office. "Time to talk to Bryan," she murmured.

If Jane had known who Bryan really was — what he was capable of — she would have understood why she couldn't shake the memory of their conversation before Christmas. The way he'd said, *"Charitable giving? Are you certain that's what it is?"* echoed relentlessly in her mind. She felt an urgency to speak with him again, to tell him that yes, there is more to John Christmas than meets the eye — she had proof. She was about to let everyone know it.

When John returned home later that afternoon, he went straight to the notepad by the phone. His eyes scanned the scrawled lines.

Jane. More info to Ellis. Sorry.

His stomach dropped. "Jane too," he whispered, the color draining from his face. *After all these years, after all the times she's stood by me...*

Mary noticed John from the kitchen, standing motionless, staring at the notepad.

"What is it?" she asked, looking over his shoulder.

He turned to face her and held up the note.

"What does that mean? I don't understand," said Mary, squinting at the paper.

"It means Jane must have been one of the employees who went to Ellis. She's taking more information to him. Maybe she thought, after all these years, the least she could do was give me a warning."

"No, John. I can't believe that. Jane would never do that," Mary replied.

"Mary, love, it says it here quite plainly," John said as he placed the notepad back by the telephone. "She seemed a little off and quiet on our walk to the train station the other day. She said she was just tired. I thought she'd feel better after a break over Christmas."

Mary frowned. "What could she be taking to Ellis?" Did you... did you do something to upset her?"

"What do you mean?" John asked defensively.

"I don't know," Mary said with a weary sigh. "I'm just trying to make sense of all of this."

"So now you're doubting me too, Mary," John snapped.

"No, no—of course not. I'm sorry. We're all on edge." Mary wrapped her arms around him.

John shut his eyes against the sting. He had trusted Jane more than anyone at Christmas Imports. And now, with a few scribbled words on a notepad, his friend—his most loyal employee seemed to have turned against him. Worse still, Mary's questions hinted that even she was beginning to doubt him. Perhaps he really was finished.

John sank into his armchair, his gaze drifting to the painting of Thomas hanging above the fireplace. Why was heaven so silent? Why was no one helping him, telling him what to do next?

Across from him, in the empty armchair, Thomas William Christmas sat watching.

"Don't give up, John. You're not as alone as you think," Thomas said softly, though his words never reached John's ears. "Heaven is rooting for you. It always has, and it always will."

AT CHRISTMAS IMPORTS, Jane rummaged through a drawer on the side of her desk and pulled out a large red book, its pages bulging with papers and notes sticking out from the top.

"If there's any doubt, this will put it to rest once and for all," she murmured, her grip tightening around the red book. She alone knew the weight of what it contained.

Holly's Gift

IT WASN'T EASY FOR Jane to get a meeting with Graham Ellis.

"Please, I need to see him," she pleaded. "I have important information about the segment he's preparing on Mr. Christmas. He won't want to miss this."

The secretary gave her a long look before sighing. "Alright. I can squeeze you in tomorrow at 10:00 a.m. For ten minutes."

The next morning, Jane sat across from Graham Ellis as he flipped through her red book, thick with papers and scribbled notes. He examined several pages closely, then closed the book with a thoughtful tap of his finger on the cover.

Graham leaned forward. "Miss Pengilly, this is good. I'd love to use it — but I can't run with notes alone. I need proof. Can you bring me witnesses?"

Jane had worried he might say that. Her throat tightened. If Graham brushed her off, the years of evidence in her red book would mean nothing. Still, she already had people in mind who could back her up. With their help, the country would know the truth about John Christmas.

"Consider it done," she said, slipping the red book back into her bag.

"But I need everything at least forty-eight hours before the segment airs — no later," Graham called after her as she reached the door.

THAT AFTERNOON JOHN went to the coat rack and put on his coat.

"I'm just popping out to get some firewood in before it gets dark," he said, buttoning it up.

He stepped into the chilly December air. Everything was still, the only sound his footsteps crunching on the frosty grass. Warm lights glowed from his neighbors' homes in the dimming afternoon light.

He paused before reaching the wood pile and looked back toward his own home. The Christmas tree glowed through the big front window, the holly wreath bright against the white door. For days now he had almost forgotten — it was still December.

He had always tried to teach his children that Christmas was a time of hope and joy. Yet he felt so hopeless and miserable. He had prayed to feel calm and happy again. But after each whispered prayer, there was nothing. Like the frosty afternoon around him, heaven itself was quiet.

As John stooped to gather logs, he felt a gentle tap on his shoulder.

"Hello, Holly-Pie," John said as he turned to see Holly. "What are you doing out here?"

"I want to give you something," she said, stepping closer.

"Oh?" John glanced up.

From beneath her coat, Holly pulled out a chain with a gold ring hanging from it — Thomas's ring. She had worn the family heirloom proudly for two years now. It was her most treasured possession.

"I want you to have this," she said, sliding the ring from the chain.

John straightened. "No, no, Holly. That's yours. I can't take it."

"Please, Daddy," she said softly. "I think it will help."

John gave a half-smile. "And how do you think it'll help?"

Holly looked at the ring in her hand. "Whenever I feel worried, or shy, or like I'm no good... I touch the ring and think about my family — about you, and Grandad, and Thomas. I remember we're Christmases, and the stories you tell every year. It reminds me who I am." She paused. "I think all those mean things people are saying have made you forget who you are. Maybe you could wear it until you remember again."

She reached up and placed the ring in his hand.

John stared at Thomas's golden ring in his palm, tears welling in his eyes. Somewhere in the distance a dog barked, breaking the silence. He looked back at Holly and smiled. Perhaps someone was listening after all.

KRAMPUS SPRAWLED ACROSS the rooftop, watching the sickly exchange between John and Holly below. It was just days now before the segment aired, and he couldn't afford for anything to go wrong. He had let himself get too distracted by the girl—*Pam,* a voice in the back of his mind corrected. He shook his head, as if to rattle her image loose.

Concentrate, fool, he growled to himself.

He had stretched himself along the entire length of the rooftop. When he took his human form of Bryan, his skin felt tight, hot, and itchy. In the beginning, he had loathed the human shell. He longed for the smoky, shadowy form of Krampus—where he could stretch and swell, slip unseen through cracks, unleash his minions to sow chaos. Bryan felt like a cage. And yet lately, he stayed in the human form more often. Against his will, he was getting used to it.

He needed to remember who he was, what he was capable of. When he was Bryan, he found himself soft and weak. He stretched out his clawed hand and made it even bigger, his claws even longer. He chuckled to himself, picturing how horrifying he would look to the humans if they saw him sprawled across the rooftop in his true form. Though he preferred to remain unseen, his invisible presence gave him the upper hand. Still, once in a while, he was tempted to let them see—remind them how monstrous he truly was. After all, it was their own warped imaginations that had shaped him into this.

Down below, John was staring at the gold ring. Krampus narrowed his eyes, focusing until the man's expression sharpened. Was that a faint glimmer of hope flickering there?

He knew whose ring it was, and he knew Thomas had been hanging around the Christmas family, meddling as usual. Oh yes, he knew Thomas William Christmas very well. For many years, Thomas had worked alongside him, Nicholas, and Martha. Cavan had always believed it was mere chance that Thomas crossed their path and became entangled in their work. Nicholas, of course, believed there was more to it.

Krampus hated the memories that crept in of those years with them. But none stung more than those from the beginning, when the world still called Nick, St. Nicholas. Back then, they were all so full of hope and optimism for the work ahead.

His lip curled. "St. Nicholas." How the world still spoke that name in reverence, as if the man had never had flaws.

He remembered the tales men still told — Nicholas sneaking bags of gold through a poor man's window to save his daughters, praying away a storm to rescue doomed sailors at sea. Always the hero. Always the saint. Cavan had been there, watching, as those miracles won Nicholas his place in the hearts of men and in Heaven itself. And now, centuries later, they still praised him for it. They could dress him up in names and titles through the ages, but to Cavan he was still just Nick.

After Thomas's death, generations of the Christmas family had remained close friends with Nicholas. That bond had all started with Thomas, and he despised it. Bringing down the

Christmas family would cut Nicholas deeper than any blade — and at last, he was close. He wasn't opposed to teaching that do-gooder angel Thomas a lesson too — rattle his hope, shake his optimism, remind him what Krampus was truly capable of.

"Nothing to worry about," he sneered, glaring at Thomas's ring in John's hand. "A dusty old trinket could never restore a ruined reputation."

"Hope makes the fall only sweeter," he hissed, before his smoky form lifted from the rooftop and slipped into the dusky sky.

'This Evening,' with Graham Ellis

"LET'S NOT WATCH THE segment tonight," Mary said gently.

"I need to," John replied, managing a sad smile. "Better to know what I'm up against before the press conference."

"Alright. We'll watch it together."

John hesitated. "I don't know, Mary love... once it airs properly, it'll all get worse."

"I can handle it," she said quietly.

"Just me and you, though." He kissed her cheek. "I can't bear for the rest of the family to see it."

"GOOD EVENING," SMILED Graham Ellis into the camera. "Before Christmas, we reported on allegations involving Christmas Imports and its owner, Mr. John Christmas..."

John's shoulders tensed.

"Questions were raised regarding Mr. Christmas's conduct in business, and indeed his character. Since then, further information has come to light. What we have discovered may well surprise you."

Please, Mary thought, her hands clenched tighter in her lap. *How can it get any worse?*

The camera panned wide, revealing Jane Pengilly seated across from Graham. She sat rigid, her posture too upright, her face pale.

John blinked. *"Jane?"*

"With me tonight is Miss Jane Pengilly, Mr. Christmas's office manager," Graham continued. "Good evening, Miss Pengilly."

Hazel, who had crept in when no one was looking, froze. Her hand shot to her mouth to muffle a gasp.

"Good evening," Jane replied, her voice just above a whisper.

"How long have you been Mr. Christmas's office manager?"

"Just over twenty years."

"Would you say you know him well?"

"Yes. Very well."

Graham's gaze flicked to a red book clenched in Jane's hands. "And what is it you've brought with you tonight?"

Jane hesitated, then gave a nervous smile. "A scrapbook... of sorts."

"And what's inside?"

"Receipts. Invoices. Letters. Things about Mr. Christmas."

The camera cut back to Graham's stern face. "Ladies and gentlemen, I've examined the papers in Miss Pengilly's book and can vouch for their authenticity."

John put his head in his hands. A tear slid down Mary's cheek.

"And why have you come forward now with this information?"

Jane looked down at the book. "Because I couldn't keep quiet any longer."

"Please tell me more about the papers and notes in your scrapbook," Graham urged.

Jane drew a breath, tilting her chin slightly. "The papers in this book prove..." Her eyes darted to Graham, then back to the camera. The studio held its breath. Then, steadier: "...that Mr. Christmas is innocent of all allegations against him."

John's head shot up. He stared at Jane on the television screen. Did he really hear that right? Did she just say *innocent of all allegations against him?* He and Mary looked at each other in disbelief.

Graham turned to the camera, his expression composed.

"That's right, ladies and gentlemen — you heard it here. On *This Evening*, we pride ourselves on uncovering the truth — and when we get it wrong, we say so. Tonight, we're doing exactly that. Miss Pengilly has come forward with new, irrefutable evidence that changes everything."

Mary jumped to her feet. "Quick, everyone — get in here!"

"Tell me more about the book, Miss Pengilly," Graham said.

Jane spoke louder now, her confidence growing. "The book shows exactly where the money went. It proves Mr. Christmas wasn't funding his own extravagant lifestyle but quietly giving company profits to good causes."

"How long have you been keeping these records?"

"For twenty years —for as long as I've worked for John Christmas."

"So, for two decades, you've kept a record of Mr. Christmas's charitable giving?"

"That's correct. Mr. Christmas always insisted on keeping his giving anonymous. Never wanted praise or recognition. As his manager, I often helped arrange things... so I was one of the few who knew."

The camera cut back to Graham. "Unfortunately — or perhaps fortunately — to clear his name, Mr Christmas's generosity can no longer remain anonymous. Why did you keep all these papers in your book, Miss Pengilly?"

Jane's expression softened. "Because I thought what John did was wonderful. I kept the book to remember the good things."

Graham nodded. "And that's not all you've done, is it?"

Jane shook her head. "No."

The family in the living room looked at each other.

"What more could there be?" Holly asked aloud.

"Ladies and gentlemen," Graham said, turning to the camera, "we have other guests with us this evening."

The camera panned to two people sitting beside Jane.

"Miss Pengilly has tracked down some of those who benefited from Mr. Christmas's generosity — people who, until recently, had no idea where their good fortune came from."

He gestured to a woman with red hair. "This is Jean Hayward. Jean, something extraordinary happened to you two years ago. Tell us about it."

Jean smiled shyly. "It was Christmas Day. I was heading home with my two children on the train. I'd lost my husband four years earlier, and money was tight. My daughter's shoes had holes in them — her feet were soaked and cold."

Graham leaned forward. "So, you're a widow, raising two children on your own?"

Jean nodded.

"What happened next?"

"I didn't know it at the time, but Mr. Christmas was on the train with his daughter. When we got off, we found a new pair of boots under my daughter's seat, right where her old shoes had been drying. I think they were Mr. Christmas's daughter's."

"That was all Holly's doing," John said proudly from his armchair.

Holly beamed; Hector rolled his eyes.

"And that wasn't the end of it, was it?" Graham prompted.

Jean shook her head, her voice cracking with quiet gratitude. "A week later, I got a letter from my local college. A whole course of evening business classes had been paid for. I didn't know it was Mr. Christmas until Miss Pengilly showed me the receipts. I'm now the manager at the hotel where I used to clean."

Graham turned back to the camera. "From cleaning rooms to running the hotel. An incredible journey. Thank you, Jean."

"My next guest is Norman Pattenden. Welcome, Norman."

The camera cut to an older man with a weathered face, one hand resting on a cane. "Thank you," he said with a gentle smile.

"You were also on the train that day, weren't you?"

"Yes. I was working. I've been a conductor on the Winchester to Waterloo line for twenty-five years."

"And when did you first meet Mr. Christmas?"

"At Waterloo station, after my shift. We walked together and chatted a bit."

"What did you talk about?"

"Oh, this and that — Christmas, the weather. But I also told him my wife had passed away the year before." His gaze dropped.

"That must have been difficult," Graham said softly.

"Very difficult," Norman said with a small nod.

"And then something happened a few months later?"

"Yes. The council contacted me about a park near my house — a place Rita, my wife, and I used to take our children. They said someone had donated new playground equipment, and a bench with a plaque. The plaque says: **In memory of Rita Pattenden.** They told me to come and see it."

"Do you go there often?"

"I go every day," Norman said, his voice thick with emotion.

"And you've only recently learned who was behind it?"

"That's right," Norman replied.

"A beautiful place to remember your wife — and a beautiful gesture from Mr. Christmas."

Hector whooped and punched the air, then quickly tried to cover his face so no one would notice his tears.

"There are hundreds more stories like this, isn't that right, Miss Pengilly?"

"Yes," said Jane. "I just opened the book to a page and contacted the first names I saw. I didn't have to look far to find proof. When John Christmas spots a worthy cause, he's there to help." She smiled and her eyes glistened.

The last guest was an employee of Christmas Imports.

"Does Mr. Christmas treat his employees well?" Graham asked Ruth Jones.

"Absolutely!" Ruth exclaimed. "He's kind, thoughtful and generous. Above fair wages and smashing Christmas parties." She grinned.

John finally let out a shaky laugh. "It was a good party."

"If you're lucky enough to land a job at Christmas Imports, you're very blessed," Ruth continued.

After a few more questions, Graham faced the camera. "From all I've seen and learned since Miss Pengilly came forward, John Christmas is a good, generous man. He owns Christmas Imports — he could use its profits for himself, but instead he helps those around him. It seems to me that Christmas Imports, and Mr. Christmas, are exactly the kind of company, and man, anyone would benefit from doing business with."

The camera zoomed in closer.

"Before Christmas, we suggested we might have a real-life Scrooge on our hands. Well... perhaps we weren't wrong — but maybe he's the other Scrooge. The one after the ghosts had done their work. The man who learned that happiness comes from helping others, not from looking after number one.

"And you know, that story is also about mistakes, forgiveness, and putting things right. Thanks to Miss Pengilly's evidence, we can say we got it wrong about Mr. Christmas. We offer our sincere apologies and hope this is the start of setting the record straight.

"From all of us at *This Evening*, Happy New Year. Here's to a kinder, better year for us all."

The living room erupted into cheers.

The Man Who Wasn't There

BRYAN—OR KRAMPUS; HE wasn't even sure which anymore—faced the choice again: stay and gloat in the Christmas home while John's segment aired, or watch it with Pam. He had waited too long to bring John Christmas down; missing his collapse felt unthinkable. And yet his time with Pam was running out. Once his work here was finished, there would be no reason to remain.

What he couldn't explain—what infuriated him—was why the thought of leaving her unsettled him at all. Each time it surfaced, it only made him angrier with himself. And then there was Mary's gaze. It always rattled him, the way she seemed to sense his presence.

He sat alone in the café, where he had sat so many times with Pam, pretending to be Bryan — the charming accountant at Christmas Imports. In the beginning, he had only come here with her. Recently, though, he had found himself dropping in on his own. Was he hoping he'd bump into her? *Idiot,* he scolded himself.

He stepped out of the café into a light drizzle and found himself walking towards Pam's flat. When she opened the door, she welcomed Bryan with a smile that lit her whole face. She was sure she would never get over the surge of excitement she felt whenever he appeared.

Two glasses of orange squash sat on coasters on the coffee table. The small black-and-white television was already humming when Bryan stepped into her living room.

They took their places on the couch at the same time, awkwardly close. Pam had never sat so near to Bryan before — at the café they always faced each other across the table. She felt the heat rise in her cheeks and her heart thud faster. Bryan glanced at her and mistook her fluster at their closeness for anxiety about the program.

"We're doing the right thing. John Christmas is getting what he deserves," he said gently.

Pam nodded and smiled.

When Jane Pengilly appeared on the television screen, Pam looked at Bryan in confusion. He went rigid, the color draining from his face.

As Graham Ellis pressed Jane with questions about her book, Pam's own spilled out in a rush.

"What's happening? Is Jane still covering for him? Did John get to her?"

Bryan didn't answer. His fists curled and uncurled in his lap, fury burning, while his eyes stayed locked on the screen. Inside, a storm raged. *Beaten again. Everything unraveling before my eyes.* He clenched his jaw so tightly it hurt. To Pam, though, he looked merely pale and stricken, as though the broadcast had knocked the wind out of him.

He had been a fool to underestimate Jane. He'd questioned her deliberately, wanting Pam to believe that Jane was covering for John — afraid of him — part of the plan. He'd been sure he'd planted enough doubt about John in her mind to keep her from becoming a problem. But now he saw he'd mistaken her kind, trusting nature for weakness. *Never underestimate the quiet one,* he thought bitterly.

Bryan suddenly rose from the couch. "I'm sorry, Pam. I never meant to hurt you." His voice was flat, and drained.

In a few long strides, he was at the door, pulling it open.

Pam jumped up, chasing after him. "Please, don't go. Let's talk and work this out."

He had heard those words before, years ago. There had been nothing to talk about then, and there was nothing to talk about now. He didn't look back. The door closed with a hollow thud that made Pam flinch.

Pam threw open the door. The hallway stretched out in both directions — long, narrow, and unnervingly still. She stepped out, her eyes darting left, then right. Every door was closed, every corridor silent. Not a single footstep, not even an echo.

"Bryan?" Her voice barely carried.

Nothing.

How could he have vanished so quickly? It was impossible. He was simply... gone — as though the man who had stood before her seconds ago had dissolved into the air, leaving not even the faintest trace behind.

The Answer Was Always in Chapter Eight

THAT NIGHT, JOHN DREAMED of Thomas.

"What good luck it was that I hired Jane," John said, smiling at him.

"Not luck," Thomas corrected gently. "It's never luck. Jane was placed in your path—not only for all the good you'd do for her, but because she would become part of the answer to all the prayers whispered on your behalf. The answer was already written into chapter eight," he added with a hint of quiet triumph.

"Chapter eight?" John repeated, confused. "What does that mean?"

Thomas winked. "Ask Holly."

"Alright," John said with a confused laugh. "I'm sure you helped to 'place Jane in my path,' as you say. After everything tonight... after coming so close to ruin... I'll never be able to thank you enough." John's voice cracked as emotion and gratitude overwhelmed him.

But Thomas shook his head. "It wasn't me this time."

John blinked. "Then who?"

"Trevor," Thomas said reverently.

"Trevor? Jane's fiancé?"

Thomas nodded. "Yes. He never really left her side."

John smiled and shook his head in wonder. The thought of Trevor watching over Jane all these years was one of the happiest comforts he could imagine.

As Thomas's image blurred, John's mind circled back to the riddle. *Chapter eight... what could it mean?* The question followed him even as his body gave in to rest. His heart, at last, was light, and he drifted into a deep, untroubled sleep.

EARLY THE NEXT MORNING, as John was getting ready for work, he spotted a white envelope on the mat by the front door. It puzzled him — there were usually several letters scattered on the mat. When he picked it up, he could tell at once it hadn't been pushed through the letterbox by the postman.

On the front, **"John Christmas"** was written in beautiful cursive handwriting. When he turned it over, a red wax seal—marked with a letter **C** intertwined with vines and leaves—gripped the flap.

Inside was a single sheet of thick, cream paper. The same looping handwriting filled the page. John didn't move from the hall as he began to read. There was no greeting — the letter started on the first line:

By now you may have some ideas about who was behind the plot to bring you down. If you guessed Bryan, you were right.

You will soon learn that Pam Roper was caught up in my designs. Do not blame her. I can be extremely persuasive — even to the strongest, most intelligent minds.

Pam was never the villain — I was. If you wish to despise someone, despise me. I twisted her into something she was never meant to be.

Well played, John Christmas. You were a worthy adversary.

The letter was unsigned — only the faint impression of the vine-entwined **C** showed through from the envelope.

After reading the note, John was even more puzzled. He had, of course, suspected Bryan — but why had he gone to all this trouble to ruin him? If they were adversaries, as the letter said, it was news to John. And if the note was from Bryan Higgin, what did the letter **C** on the wax seal stand for?

It had been several days since John asked Terrance to look into Bryan. Between preparing for a possible press conference and dreading the segment, he hadn't followed up. *I need to ring Terrance when I get into the office,* he thought. *Maybe he can make more sense of this.*

John was still standing in the hall when Holly came down the stairs, sleepy-eyed.

"Good morning, sunshine," John said brightly.

A smile lit up Holly's whole face. Her dad was finally his old self again — happy, whistling in the morning, telling silly jokes. The world felt right.

"Good morning," she replied.

"I want you to have Thomas's ring back," John said, trying to keep his voice steady. He pulled it out of his suit pocket and gently placed it in Holly's hand. "Thank you for helping me remember all that it means to be a part of the Christmas family."

Holly closed her hand around the ring, holding the family treasure safe in her small fist. She wrapped her arms around her dad and held on as tightly as she could.

"Oh, and when I get home tonight, you need to tell me what chapter eight is about," John said, kissing the top of her head.

The answer was always in chapter eight, Thomas's words whispered through her mind.

How did Dad know about Thomas — and Chapter eight?

The Christmas Ledger

JOHN OPENED THE OFFICE door at Christmas Imports. So much had changed since he had last stepped into this room. Yet, everything looked the same, still in its place, just as he had left it before the holidays. Had it really only been two weeks ago?

A soft knock pulled John from his thoughts.

"Come in," he called.

The door swung open and there stood Jane, her grin stretching from ear to ear.

They had spoken briefly on the telephone after the broadcast, but this was the first time they had met in person since the day John had walked her to the train station.

John crossed the room in two strides and pulled her into a hug so tight she laughed against his shoulder.

"Easy there, Mr. Christmas," she teased.

"I'm just so happy to see you — and I can't thank you enough," John said, laughing and crying all at once. He guided her to a chair. "Come, sit, sit."

Taking his place behind the desk, he shook his head in wonder. "I really thought you'd turned on me, Jane. I thought you were the last nail in my coffin."

Jane folded her arms. "I still don't understand why you thought that. And frankly, I'm upset you'd think I'd betray you."

"I know, I know. There was a message Hazel took that didn't make sense, and you seemed a little off at the train station. I wasn't thinking straight," he admitted with an apologetic smile.

Jane gave an understanding nod. "It was Bryan, you know — he was behind all of this."

"Yes, I know. But how did you realize it was him?" John asked.

"He came to me before Christmas asking questions about the books. He made me feel very uneasy. I never dreamed he'd go as far as he did, though. After I saw the teaser, I tried to reach him, but all the information he gave us was false. No working telephone, no real address. It's like he's a ghost."

John's eyebrows rose. "That's very strange."

"Then I went to see Pam after the broadcast. I knew Bryan and Pam were friendly, and I thought she might be able to get hold of him. But she said the same thing — he just vanished after the broadcast. Then she admitted it was the two of them who went to Ellis. She feels awful."

John nodded slowly. "I got a letter this morning from Bryan, saying much the same thing."

"Really?" Jane's voice rose in surprise.

"Yes. He said not to blame Pam — claimed he can be very persuasive."

Jane tapped her finger on the arm of the chair. "Interesting. Well, maybe Bryan actually did something good at last. Because I agree — you can't blame Pam. In fact, I think she should be commended."

John sat up straighter. "I expected you might tell me to forgive her. But commend her?"

"Bryan laid the groundwork for months. He had pages of outrageous notes about you and slipped in little digs whenever he could. She wasn't here long enough to know it was nonsense — and let's be honest, even some of your longtime employees believed the teaser at first."

"True," John admitted, remembering the phone calls.

"Bryan was good at convincing people — you saw it yourself, how quick and charming he was. Pam believed him completely. And when she thought you were in the wrong, she didn't stay quiet. She spoke up. Misguided, yes — but it still took courage, John. And integrity."

John leaned back, thoughtful. "Hmmm. I'd never thought of it like that. Well, I'm sure it took you plenty of courage too, going to the great Graham Ellis and telling him he was wrong."

Jane laughed.

John rested his hands on the desk and sighed. After days of tension locked in his body, he was still relishing the sweet feeling of relief. "I just can't believe you kept all that paperwork. I had no idea. Jane Pengilly and her red book save the day," he said with a grin.

"I think of it now as John Christmas's ledger," Jane said softly. "The company ledger may have caused some of this trouble, but my red book — that's the true record. It shows who you really are."

John smiled, a little embarrassed but deeply moved. For a moment, neither of them spoke, both lost in their own thoughts of all that had happened in the past few days.

"You were always so insistent on keeping things quiet," Jane said with a faint smile. "I couldn't tell you — not without risking you'd be cross with me."

John shook his head. "How could I ever be cross with you? I owe you everything."

Jane lowered her gaze to her hands, unsure of how to respond. Finally, she looked up again. "Since you're singing my praises, perhaps now's a good time to tell you something. You were right about the train station. I was a little off that day. I've been working up the courage to tell you something for a while now."

John's voice rose in alarm, the familiar tension returning. "What is it? Is something wrong?"

Jane shook her head. "No, no — nothing's wrong. I just... I think it's time for me to retire."

John froze. "What? No. I don't know how I'd run this place without you."

"John, calm down. I'm not about to leave you stranded. I have an idea."

"But Jane—"

She lifted a hand to stop him. "Listen, John. I'm just tired. It's time to slow down."

John's eyes widened, a cold prickle running down his spine. "You're not ill, are you?"

"No," Jane said quickly. Then, more softly: "But even if I were... perhaps it wouldn't be so terrible. I haven't seen Trevor in a very long time." Her eyes glistened.

John paused, remembering his dream from the night before. "Ah, Trevor," he said, a knowing smile returning to his face.

Jane nodded once, then shook off the brief moment of sadness. "Anyway — enough about me. Let me tell you about my idea." Her voice brightened again.

"Alright," John said hopefully. "What's your idea?"

JOHN KNOCKED FIRMLY on Pam's flat door. No answer. He knocked again, harder this time. He knew she was home — he could hear the muffled sound of voices through the door, the television, he guessed. He would stand here all night if he had to. He had something to say, and he wouldn't leave until it was said.

At last, the door opened. Pam's eyes widened.

"Mr. Christmas," she stammered.

"Hello, Pam. Do you have a minute?"

"Yes," she said quickly. "Would you like to come in?"

"No, thank you. This won't take long."

She nodded, clasping her hands together.

"You weren't at work today," John said.

Pam blinked. "Well, no. I was certain I didn't have a job anymore at Christmas Imports."

"Why would you think that?"

"You mean... you don't know? You don't know that it was me and Bryan who went to Graham Ellis?" She lowered her gaze, unable to meet his eyes.

"Yes, I know," John said gently. "That's why I want you to come back. Not only that — I'm offering you a promotion and a good pay increase." He smiled warmly, which only baffled her more.

Pam gave a nervous laugh. "Is this a joke, Mr. Christmas? After what I did? How could you possibly want me back?"

"Because I need someone like you to take Jane's place. She's retiring."

Pam shook her head slowly. "I don't understand."

"Look, Pam. You truly believed those things about me. And if they had been true — about me, or about anyone — I'd want someone to speak up. I respect people who stand up for what's right. So, I'd like you to come and help me run Christmas Imports."

A tear slid down her cheek. "I don't know what to say."

"Say yes," John replied simply.

"Yes," she whispered.

"Good. We'll see you tomorrow. Jane will start training you. It was her idea, by the way," John added with a small laugh.

Pam watched as he turned to leave, then called out, "Mr. Christmas." John turned around.

"A woman came to see me a few days ago, said her name is Martha. She said she's Bryan's sister. She told me she wasn't making excuses, but that he had his reasons. She said... maybe

I could forgive him someday. I didn't think I ever could. But if you can forgive me... well, perhaps, maybe one day I can."

John straightened. His voice was quiet but steady. "Forgiveness is a wonderful thing." He gave her a final nod, then walked away.

Pam stood frozen in the doorway long after his footsteps faded. The television still hummed behind her, but she barely heard it. Relief and shame wrestled inside her — relief at John's mercy, shame at how easily she had been swayed by Bryan.

Forgiveness is a wonderful thing. John's words echoed in her mind. Could she forgive Bryan?

She closed the door slowly and leaned against it. She had been given another chance. But did Bryan deserve one too?

The Ghost Accountant

"HELLO, JOHN!" TERRANCE'S voice came through the line bright and cheerful.

The last few telephone conversations between them had been tense and somber, but now Terrance sounded undeniably upbeat.

"Hello, Terrance."

"Congratulations, John. What an absolutely splendid outcome to all that nonsense."

"Yes. I can still hardly believe it. I feel incredibly blessed." John let out a long breath of relief.

Terrance chuckled. "Well, if anyone deserves some good fortune, it's you."

"Thank you, that means a lot. The reason I'm ringing is to ask what you found out about Bryan Higgin." Even speaking the name made the old tension creep back into his body.

"Ah, yes. I told you I'd call if we uncovered anything. But the truth is, John, we've found nothing. His entire CV was fabricated. There's no record of him anywhere. We rang his references — all the numbers were disconnected. No birth certificate, no tax records, not even a police record. Nothing. It's like he's a ghost."

Jane had said those exact words about him: *like he's a ghost.*

"Very strange," John murmured.

"It gets even stranger," Terrance went on. "I had one of my chaps search the office he'd been using at Christmas Imports. Nothing personal left behind, not even a mug. But he did find eight months of uncashed paychecks."

"He didn't take any pay the entire time he worked here?" John asked.

"It seems that way," Terrance replied.

"We'll keep digging and let you know if anything turns up. Also, John..." He paused. "May I offer you a bit of friendly advice — as your legal counsel, but also as your friend?"

"Of course, Terrance."

"I know you like a friendly atmosphere at Christmas Imports, and I'm not saying you should change that. But perhaps it's time to tighten things up — account for every penny, check new employees more carefully. Unfortunately, it's just part of the modern world we live in."

"Thank you, Terrance, you're right. I appreciate the advice."

JOHN OPENED THE DOOR to Bryan's office. A chill, damp smell hit him immediately. He flicked on the desk lamp; the bulb flickered to life, buzzing faintly as its weak glow barely lit the room.

What was he doing in here all those months? And why here? Why this depressing, cave-like room?

Bryan had always come across as charming, warm, and kind — to him, at least. But this bleak, dim room felt like a glimpse of the parts of Bryan's soul he had kept hidden.

He opened the desk drawer and stared at the pile of uncashed checks. Would he ever understand what drove Bryan to spend nearly a year plotting and scheming to bring him down?

John stacked the checks in his hand. The paper felt cold, smelling of must and dust from months in the drawer. What sort of man worked for almost a year with no thought of money? Whatever Bryan's motives were, they hadn't been greed. That thought bothered John even more.

He hurried out to the main office floor. The air there felt lighter, but he couldn't shake the bleakness clinging to him from Bryan's office.

"Could you please total these checks and write a new one out to King's College of London?" John asked a junior accountant.

The young man looked at him, startled, but then nodded quickly.

Some things might have to change at Christmas Imports — but not everything.

JOHN HANDED A CHECK for one thousand three hundred pounds to the treasurer at King's College. "Please use this to fund the tuition of a deserving student," he said. "Perhaps someone in your accounting department. We could use more good accountants in the business world."

The treasurer adjusted his glasses, staring at the sum written neatly across the page. For a moment he seemed at a loss for words.

"That's... very generous of you, Sir. This would actually be enough to cover tuition for several students."

John gave a modest smile. "Then I'll leave it in your good hands to find them." He started to walk away, then paused and turned back. "And if I might trouble you for a receipt, please?"

The treasurer nodded, still staring at the check. John walked out into the wintry air. He took a deep breath and straightened his shoulders. Each step away from Bryan—the ghost accountant—felt like a step back into the light.

A January Thanksgiving

AFTER DINNER THAT EVENING, John leaned back in his chair and folded his arms. *Family, good food, and peace at last. Life doesn't get much better,* he thought with a smile, looking around the table at his loved ones. For that moment, everything felt perfect — and how thankful he was!

That reminded him of something. "You know, Mary love, we have an American client..."

"An American?" Hazel said eagerly, her head shooting up from her plate. "How old is he?"

"What?" John blinked, confused. "I don't know. Probably around my age, I'd guess."

"Oh." Hazel's enthusiasm faded. "So, really old then."

Hector, who was helping himself to another scoop of mashed potatoes, smirked. "What did you think—that Dad's American client looks like Elvis Presley?" he jeered.

Holly giggled.

"Anyway," John went on, "before Christmas he told me they celebrate a holiday over there called Thanksgiving."

"Oh yes, I've heard of that," Mary said.

"It's a bit like our harvest festivals," John explained. "Celebrating the harvest and giving thanks."

Mary nodded.

"My client said they have a big meal with family and friends and then everyone says what they're grateful for afterwards."

"That's lovely," Mary said with a smile.

"I've just been thinking how grateful I am," John said, emotion creeping into his voice. "I didn't know if our family would ever be the same again. But I feel we're stronger than ever now. The business is thriving, Jane says people are practically banging down the doors to work with us. And I'm so thankful for the loyalty of Jane and Terrance. I could go on and on."

"There's definitely a lot to be thankful for," Mary agreed, patting his hand.

By now Hector had wiped his plate clean and was slowly edging away from the table. He was glad his dad's name had been cleared, but he didn't feel like sitting here for another one of Dad's thankful speeches.

"Not so fast, mister," John said. "This is the part you'll like."

Hector slumped back into his chair with a quiet huff.

"So, I was thinking—how about we have a Thanksgiving here, in January?" John said brightly.

"Oh yes, that sounds lovely, John. But I don't really know what to do. How do we do it?" Mary asked.

"We just put on a dinner—turkey and all the trimmings. Invite family and friends. Maybe Jane and Terrance and his wife. And then after the meal we'll each say what we're thankful for."

"Ooo, I'm going to make a list!" Holly said, clapping her hands together.

Hector rolled his eyes at Holly. "Will there be sweets?" he asked, suddenly more interested.

"Yes, yes," John said. "They have pies—lots of them. We'll bake every kind. You can never have too many pies," he added with a wink.

Hector pictured the table in front of him full of pies. *Maybe this Thanksgiving idea wasn't so bad after all.*

Between Light and Shadow

BRYAN SAT IN THE CAFÉ in his usual seat. The place looked the same, the staff were the same two chatty ladies, but it felt unbearably different. The real difference, of course, was that Pam was not across from him — tucking her hair behind her ear, sharing office gossip, smelling faintly of strawberry shampoo. Even the custard tarts tasted different.

He set his half-eaten tart back on the plate. Why had he come back to this ridiculous place? He had lived for years as Krampus, with one clear purpose: ruin Christmas. Now, after failing with the Christmas family twice, he didn't know who he was anymore. And to make his wretched life even more miserable, he couldn't get Pam out of his head.

A tap on his shoulder made him stiffen. His heart leapt — then fell. It wasn't Pam. But the smiling face was just as familiar.

"Martha! What are you doing here?"

"Aren't you going to offer me a seat?" she asked.

He gestured to Pam's empty chair. "Of course. Sit."

Martha slipped off her coat. "How are you?"

"I've been better," he admitted with a sad smile.

"So I hear. You stirred up a lot of trouble this time."

Bryan looked down. They sat quietly for a moment.

"Pam's nice," Martha said casually, breaking the silence.

Bryan looked up sharply. "You know about Pam?"

"Of course. Did you forget who I answer to?" She pointed upward.

He sighed, staring at the tart again.

"Maybe it's not too late, Cavan — or Bryan. You've got more names than Nicholas now, but I'm certainly not calling you Krampus."

"I don't think I'm Cavan or Krampus anymore. Bryan will do." It was the name Pam had known him by. For some reason, it was the one he wanted to keep.

Martha patted his hand. "Alright, Bryan. I know you like her. Maybe you should tell her."

He snorted. "Oh yes, right. I'll just knock on her door and say, 'Hello, Pam, remember me? The liar who manipulated you? It turns out I can't stop thinking about you. Fancy a custard tart?'" His mouth twisted into a bitter smile.

"You'll never know unless you try," Martha said with a shrug.

"She doesn't know me — who I truly am," Bryan murmured.

"Bryan is closer to the true you than Krampus," Martha said with a small smile. "Pam fell for your charm and humor, your thoughtfulness. That's the real you. Go and talk to her."

Go and talk to her. Could it really be that simple?

Martha pulled a folded piece of paper from her coat pocket. She laid it flat on the table in front of him. A charcoal sketch stared back at him — his own face, drawn with care.

"You drew this?" he asked, staring at the likeness.

Martha nodded. "This is who you've always been to me," she said, smoothing the creases. "You can call yourself Cavan, or Krampus, or Bryan — but to me, you're the tender-hearted man who never wanted to disappoint the children. The one who only ever wanted to be loved and accepted."

Martha always gave him more grace than he had ever deserved.

She rose, slipping her coat back on, and left him with thoughts he had never dared to imagine. The café door closed softly behind her. She glanced back through the window for a final look. For a moment she saw Cavan. Then she corrected herself: Bryan. He sat where she had left him, caught between past and future, light and shadow.

Somewhere in the distance, Big Ben struck ten o'clock. Time ran differently for the likes of her, Bryan, and Nicholas — but she had seen time reshape places and people alike. She had watched babies grow into rulers, empires crumble into dust, and valleys lift into mountains. If time could do all of that, perhaps it could turn a villain back into a hero.

As she walked down the wet cobblestone high street a banner in a shop front window caught her eye. '*Happy New Year,*' it read. New years always brought with them the promise of change and hope. Not only was this a new year, but a new decade. On this grey January afternoon in London, Martha felt full of hope — and for now, that light was enough.

Also by Sarah Phillips

Holly's Christmas Quest
Hector's Christmas Knight
The Christmas Ledger

About the Author

Sarah Phillips was born on a snowy Christmas Day in Portsmouth, England — a fitting beginning for someone whose stories would one day celebrate the spirit of Christmas.

She married her husband, Matthew, in 1989, and together they have lived in both England and the United States. She is a happy wife, mother of four, and now mother-in-law to two.

As a breast cancer survivor, Sarah believes deeply in hope, resilience, and the power of second chances — themes that often shine through in her writing.